Addicted to the Drama 2

Jamila

Lock Down Publications and Ca$h
Presents
Addicted to the Drama 2
A Novel by *Jamila*

Addicted to the Drama 2

Lock Down Publications
P.O. Box 870494
Mesquite, Tx 75187

Visit us at
www.lockdownpublications.com

Lock Down Publications
Like our page on Facebook: Lock Down Publications @
www.facebook.com/lockdownpublications.ldp
Cover design and layout by: **Dynasty Cover Me**
Book interior design by: **Shawn Walker**
Edited by: **Sunny Giovanni**

Jamila

Stay Connected with Us!

Addicted to the Drama 2

Submission Guideline

Submit the first three chapters of your completed manuscript to ldpsubmissions@gmail.com, subject line: Your book's title. The manuscript must be in a .doc file and sent as an attachment. Document should be in Times New Roman, double spaced and in size 12 font. Also, provide your synopsis and full contact information. If sending multiple submissions, they must each be in a separate email.

Have a story but no way to send it electronically? You can still submit to LDP/Ca$h Presents. Send in the first three chapters, written or typed, of your completed manuscript to:

LDP: Submissions Dept
P.O. Box 870494
Mesquite, Tx 75187

DO NOT send original manuscript. Must be a duplicate.

Provide your synopsis and a cover letter containing your full contact information.

Thanks for considering LDP and Ca$h Presents.

Jamila

Acknowledgements

First, I like to thank God for helping me discover my talent in writing and guiding me through this difficult but rewarding journey. I like to thank my family and fiends for their never-ending love and support. I want to give a shout out to my fellow alumni and the current students of Dougherty Comprehensive High School of Albany, Georgia and Savannah State University of Savannah, Georgia. I also want to thank my readers who have been with me since day one during my Cynthia Blue days (Don't worry I'll finish the Bryson Blood Wars Series LOL!). You guys are my everything! I appreciate you giving my books a chance, giving me feedback and encouraging me to keep pushing. I also want to thank my CBC family for giving me a chance even though things didn't quite work out, but hey things happen. Thank you Nyeshia, The Cunning Linguist and Paradise Taylor. Last but not least I like to thank my beloved C.E.O. Ca$h aka Big Sweetie Who Never Smiles (That's my pet name for him LOL!). Thanks for giving me this opportunity to join LDP. I hope I make you proud and I hope we have a long, flourishing and successful professional relationship and make big things happen in this industry. Also, to my beloved C.O.O. Coffee thanks for the kind words and encouragement. Your professionalism, optimism and highly positive attitude have opened my eyes on so many levels. You are one of the very few people I've met who delivers harsh criticism and still be sweet and gentle. It makes it hard to argue LOL! Thanks Ca$h and Coffee for opening your doors to me and the rest of the LDP family for making me feel welcome and I hope y'all like the second installment of this romantic drama as much as y'all liked Part One. Enjoy! *hugs and kisses*

Dedication

Reico Lamont Welch

B.K.A.

R.L. Welch

February 22, 1976 – November 19, 2016

I like to dedicate this project to the man who gave me my very first chance in this industry. Thanks, Reico, for giving my pen a chance under your publishing company G-Princess Publishing and helping me get my foot in the door. No matter how far I travel down this road in my literary journey I'll always carry your wisdom with me.

Jamila

Addicted to the Drama 2

Chapter 1

"Oh, shit." Macal, grunted as he was hitting Lolette's pussy from the back.

"Ah—shit." Lolette panted, holding onto the edge of the bed for dear life, loving every minute of Macal, pounding her pussy with her ass in the air.

Macal's room phone rang. He ignored it and kept making Lolette's pussy sore and creamy. Lolette made her ass clap and took the dick like a champ. Then, Macal's smartphone rang.

"You want to answer that?" Lolette asked between moans.

"Fuck that phone." Macal breathed, feeling Lolette's pussy tighten around his dick, not paying attention to his phone on the nightstand, that had Thuy's picture flashing on the caller I.D.

****

Thuy took the elevator down to the second floor where Macal's room was. She walked down the hall, trying to find Macal's room.

"Thuy, is that you?" Tylisha asked when she saw her walk by.

Thuy turned around and saw Tylisha and Enzo, arm and arm, dressed to kill. "Tylisha—Enzo, what's up?" Thuy pulled them into a group hug.

"What brings you here?" Tylisha asked.

"Didn't your brother tell you? I'm here on business this week," Thuy answered. "Actually, we kind of surprised each other. He told me about this hotel, and I decided to check it out for myself. Where are the kids?"

"Playing laser tag," Enzo answered. "We're heading out to check out some of the clubs."

"I'm trying to find Macal's room," Thuy said. "I know it's on this floor."

"Oh, it's down the hall. Make a right, it's the very first door on the left." Tylisha pointed down the hall to the left, giving Thuy the directions.

"Thanks, have fun."

"See ya."

Thuy followed the directions, headed straight for Macal's room all smiles. The closer she got to the door, the happier she became. Thuy couldn't wait to see Macal's face and continue their blossoming courtship. She felt like a little girl on Christmas morning. She approached his door and pulled the keycard out of her purse. She slid the keycard in the slot to unlock the door, opened it, and let herself inside the suite. To her surprise, Macal, was nowhere to be found, but she knew he had been there. The T.V. was on and his luggage was in plain sight.

Thuy walked around the room calling his name. "Macal— Macal!" When she past the bathroom door, she heard the shower running and concluded that's where he was. "No wonder he didn't hear me when I called." She knocked on the bathroom door and said. "Macal, it's Thuy, I'm here."

"Alright baby, make yourself at home!" He yelled back.

Thuy giggled and said to herself. "He called me baby." She found the remote on the nightstand, sat on the couch, and started flipping through the channels.

Thuy was then surprised by a kiss on the cheek. "You made it baby girl," Macal, said with cheer.

"Of course, I did." Thuy said, scanning the luxurious suite, and the sexy live milk chocolate specimen wearing his pajama bottoms, giving her a clear view of his dick print. "Nice place."

"Yes, it is."

"How are you loving New Orleans, so far?"

"Now that you're here it's great." Macal pulled Thuy off the couch and gave her a rough wet kiss.

"Oh Macal, all this flattering almost makes me wanna give you some pussy right now."

Hearing those words made Macal slowly reach into his pajama bottoms to pull his dick out.

Thuy stopped him by saying, "Almost."

Macal, took his hand out of his pants with no argument. "That's cool."

"You know I'm not quite ready for that yet."

Ever since the Jeromy incident, Thuy had been very cautious when it came to sex, even though deep down she wanted Macal deep inside her.

It was like her pussy was saying, *Bitch is you crazy? He's your nigga, he's fine, sexy as fuck, and his ass is packing. Take that thong off, get in that bed, legs wide or face down ass up, and let that nigga fuck.*

Thuy's mind however, was saying, *Don't listen to that fast, nasty ass hoe. Take your time and see what this dude is all about. Make him earn the pussy.*

Thuy decided to listen to her mind instead of her pussy.

"I can respect that." Macal understood where Thuy was coming from. He didn't want to make her feel uncomfortable. "I was just kidding. I don't wanna pressure you to do something you're not ready for. I just like being with you."

"Awe Macal, I like being with you too." Thuy planted a kiss on his lips and saw the T.V. lineup flash on the screen. "Oh shit. *Mommie Dearest* is coming on in about an hour."

"*Mommie Dearest*?" Macal asked.

"Yes, it's my favorite movie of all time." Thuy cheered.

"*Mommie Dearest*? I never seen it, but I heard of it before. Isn't it based on a true story, about a movie star from back in the day, who adopted some kids and abused them?" Macal reminded himself.

"Yeah, *Joan Crawford*." Thuy confirmed Macal's answer. "The daughter *Christina Crawford* wrote a book about her childhood and it became a movie."

"She wrote about her experiences and shared them with the world. That's amazing." Macal commended.

"I always admire people brave enough to go there. I think we can learn a lot from them. That's why *Mommie Dearest* is my favorite movie. I admire Christina's guts." Suddenly a light bulb flashed inside Thuy's head. "I have an idea. Let's get in our pajamas, order room service, and watch the movie here."

"Great idea and *My Fellow Americans* comes on after *Mommie*

Dearest." Macal mentioned, pointing at the T.V.

"You like that movie, too?" Thuy asked with amazement.

"Hell yeah. That shit was funny."

"I haven't seen that movie in years. Let me shower, change, and pack my overnight bag. I'll be right back for our private slumber party." Thuy said.

"Take your time baby." Macal said as Thuy walked out the door.

"Bye for now." Thuy said.

"Bye for now, too, baby." Macal said.

They kept saying goodbye to each other, being silly as Thuy walked down the hallway.

"You." Thuy giggled as she slowly walked backwards down the hall.

"No, you." Macal grinned while still standing in the doorway.

"Oh yeah, you." Thuy pointed at Macal.

"Oh, you—you—you—you." Macal blew air kisses and rubbed his crotch.

"Nigga, you silly." Thuy laughed.

"Girl." Macal laughed, when he couldn't see Thuy anymore he closed the door behind him.

He leaned on the door and took a deep breath, with a big smile on his face. He looked over at the closet, walked towards it, to open the door.

He yanked a half-naked, Lolette, out of the closet, she was pissed the fuck off. "Nigga who the fuck was that?" She wanted answers now.

"Shh, hurry up, and get out." Macal ignored Lolette's question and pulled her out of the door.

"You kicking my ass out for that—"

"I'll call you when I get back to Atlanta. Take your ticket and get on the next plane back home."

"But—" Lolette was cut off by a door slam to the face.

****

Addicted to the Drama 2

Thuy showered, put on her form-fitting baby blue *Victoria's Secret* pink pajamas, with the cami top, matching robe, and bedroom slippers. Then she packed her overnight *Dolce & Gabanna* bag and made her way back to the second floor.

Thuy was so happy, she was practically skipping down the hall to Macal's room. During her merriment stroll, a half-naked woman deliberately brushed past her, almost knocking her down without so much as an excuse me or an apology.

What the fuck? Thuy turned around, barely catching a quick glance at the woman's face. Her facial features were familiar. *Where have I seen that bitch before?*

Thuy brushed it off and went on to see her man.

"Fuck that rude ass bitch." She mumbled, approaching Macal's door and knocked.

"You made it, my lady." Macal greeted, taking Thuy's hand, leading her inside.

"Of course." Thuy said.

Macal took her bag. She looked at the spread of food Macal ordered. There were wings, chips. Pepsi, finger sandwiches, and a cooler full of Heinekens.

"Oh shit. You went all out up in here. All this food and drinks."

"My black ass was hungry." Macal justified.

"You and me both."

Thuy glanced over to her left, seeing something very suspicious. "What the fuck is that?"

"What's wrong baby?"

"Over there by the nightstand." She pointed, where the nightstand was located. "Is that a rainbow colored thong?"

That bitch. Macal knew what Lolette was trying to pull.

He knew for a fact, that thong was not there when Thuy came to the room the first time. If her ass wanna play motherfucking games he could play too. He had something for that ass, but first things first.

"You have a good eye. I wouldn't have noticed. A past guest must've left that, and housekeeping must've missed it."

"It happens." Thuy nodded. "One time I was at a hotel in New

York for a fashion show, I was invited to. I found a used condom in the sink." She shared.

"Ew, that shit is gross." Macal exclaimed in disgust.

"Tell me about it." Thuy said.

After Macal threw the thong away they fixed their plates.

"The movie is starting."

Macal and Thuy, sat on the couch with their plates.

"Let's dig in and check this movie out." Macal said and proceeded to enjoy a night of great cinema with his priceless lady.

Addicted to the Drama 2

Chapter 2

May 2, 1993

Rufus continued kissing Taryn, then laid her down on the bed, undressing her.

"That bastard." Macal whispered.

He was old enough to know what was going to happen next. Rufus was getting undressed, while Taryn positioned herself on the bed on all fours, with her ass in the air.

The sight of Taryn's nude body made Macal's dick rock hard. It was very disturbing, getting a hard-on from the woman who'd made his mother's life a living hell, and who was the cause of turmoil in his family, but he couldn't help it.

Taryn was a beautiful, sexy woman. Her dark brown, bedroom eyes, matched her beautiful face. Her chestnut skin made her body even sexier. Her melon titties bounced up and down. Rufus pounding her pussy from the back was all Macal could take. Watching Rufus tear up the pussy, holding that big, juicy ass for dear life, made Macal sick and jealous.

This man was betraying his beloved mother in their house, in their bed, but at the same time, he wanted to know what that pussy felt like on his dick. Macal, was squeezing his dick through his shorts, getting turned on by Taryn moaning with pleasure, taking the dick like a champ. Yes, Macal hated her, but he couldn't help lusting over her.

Rufus took his dick out of Taryn, she spread her legs, exposing her neatly trimmed, dripping wet pussy.

Macal almost fainted. She's got a pretty pussy. He thought.

She took one of her hands and began rubbing her clit, then used her other hand to put Rufus's dick in her mouth. Taryn's dick sucking skills, impressed Macal. She sucked on it like she was setting a world record.

When it was Rufus's turn to give Taryn oral. Macal, regained his composure, he wanted to go straight to his room and jack off, hoping it would get his mind off wanting to fuck the shit out of his

Jamila

father's mistress.

He turned around and bumped into Tylisha. "How long have you been standing there?" Macal asked, hoping Tylisha, didn't see what Rufus and Taryn were doing, let, alone what he was doing.

"Just now," Tylisha answered.

Macal, sighed with relief, pulled Tylisha by her hand, and went back downstairs. "I thought I told you to do your homework."

"My homework is finished. Now I want to help you," Tylisha said.

"Tylisha you need to stay out of this," Macal said.

This was one fucked up situation. Finding out his father was even a bigger trifling nigga than he thought. He was up there fucking his main hoe, in the bed he shared with his mother. While Macal wished that was him up there tearing up Taryn's walls instead. Macal didn't know what to do. He glanced at the phone, picked it up, and dialed the number.

****

"These pictures are great." Belinda looked through Gladys' vacation pictures, sitting around Doris' living room. "You and Harry, must've had a great time in Biloxi."

"Yes, we did." Gladys said. "He knows how much I love casinos."

"We know girl." Doris said. "We know to you winning the jackpot, is better than cumming!"

"And Harry made me do plenty of that." Gladys blushed.

"La—la—la—la—la!" Belinda playfully tried to drown out her mom and her best friend's sex talk, while covering her ears.

"Oh sorry, baby." Doris apologized, kissing Belinda on the cheek. The phone rang, "I'll get it." She went into the kitchen to answer the phone. "Hello!"

"Hi Grandma Doris." Macal greeted.

"Macal, baby, how are things?"

"I need to talk to momma."

"Alright baby." Doris took the phone off her ear and yelled.

16

"Belinda, it's Macal."

"I'll be right back, Gladys." Belinda handed the pictures back to Gladys and went into the kitchen. Doris gave her the phone. "What's up, baby?"

"Momma, I'm sorry. I didn't know what to do, so I called you." Macal said with worry.

"What's wrong, baby?" Belinda was deeply concerned.

"Taryn's here." Macal said.

"What?" Hearing that name triggered something inside Belinda. She thought she'd heard the last of that bitch.

Macal didn't know how to sugarcoat the situation, so he blurted out the first thing that popped in his head. "She was looking for dad. I didn't really want to tell her where he was. She pushed me out of the way, knocking me against the grandfather clock, letting herself in the house. My arm was a little sore but I'm alright...."

Belinda didn't need to hear anything else. The hoe coming into her home, putting her hands, on her child was enough for her.

****

Macal looked at the phone in his hand in disbelief. He couldn't believe what he'd just done.

"What did momma say?" Tylisha asked.

"She just hung up."

Tylisha had a pretty good idea what was about to happen. "Momma's on her way home, isn't she?"

Macal looked up and could still hear the sounds of Rufus and Taryn's lustful adulterous fucking coming from the bedroom upstairs. He shook his head at the inevitable. "I'm afraid so Tylisha— I'm afraid so."

****

Macal jumped off the couch in a panic. "Fuck. Why the fuck did I make that call?" He walked over to the cooler to grab himself a Heineken. "Shit."

Jamila

"Macal what's the matter?" Thuy asked with a yawn.

"I'm sorry baby. I didn't mean to wake you." Macal apologized and grabbed another Heineken for Thuy and took his seat back on the couch next to her.

"That must've been some nightmare." Thuy assumed watching Macal open the beer bottles.

"You don't know the half of it." Macal sighed, handing Thuy her beer.

"Do you mind if I ask what your dream was about?"

"May second, nineteen ninety-three."

"I get it. You were dreaming about your momma's accident." Thuy held Macal's hand and kissed it. "It's okay, I know it hurts."

"You don't understand." Macal shook his head.

"You're right. I haven't been in your shoes. I didn't mean to offend you."

"Baby, I didn't mean it like that." Macal gently caressed Thuy's beautiful face. "You know momma died in a freak accident. But what you don't know, is that it was all my fault."

"Macal you shouldn't say things like that. You were a teenage boy. I know you loved your mother and wanted to protect her, but you shouldn't feel guilty." Then something dawned on Thuy. "I noticed something. You talk about your mother's death, but never your father's death. What happened to him?"

Macal rarely discussed his father. As far as he was concerned, he didn't owe his ass the memory. "I don't really share this, but okay. You know my dad fucked around on my momma, right?"

"Right."

Macal continued. "His main side bitch was a hoe named Taryn. She really gave momma hell. As far back as I can remember. One of those altercations caused momma to go into premature labor with Tylisha."

"Shit, that was one vicious bitch!" Thuy said.

"Tell me about it." Macal agreed. "She always accused momma of stealing dad from her and trapping him."

"Why?"

"Dad and Taryn were dating first. Then he started dating

18

momma right after they broke up. Of course he never stopped fucking Taryn. Somewhere down the line momma told dad about a surprise coming soon. The news of the surprise motivated dad to propose to momma, and they went straight to the courthouse to get married. Eight months later the surprise showed up." Macal flashed a big smile implying that he was the surprise.

"Awe you was an unplanned miracle baby too, huh?" Thuy replied with a big smile of her own. "Being younger than my dad's marriage to another woman was a dead giveaway for me."

"My birthday being eight months after my parents wedding anniversary was a big clue for me." Macal added.

The two sipped their beers, then Thuy spoke again. "Oh, I see. Taryn thought your momma used her pregnancy with you to steal her man and the affair didn't stop after your folks got married."

Macal nodded, confirming Thuy's accurate guess. "When I was thirteen and Tylisha was seven, Taryn ended up pregnant."

Thuy had seen this scene one too many times. She knew exactly where Macal was going with this. "Your daddy was the father?"

"Correct." Macal replied. "She threw it in momma's face, of course. Being the lying bastard dad was, he denied everything, and momma believed him for some reason. Momma cut back on her drinking and their marriage was back on track. Meanwhile he told Taryn, that if she aborted the baby he'd leave momma and marry her."

"In other words, your daddy pulled a Jeromy?"

"You got it."

Thuy took another sip of her beer. "I don't know why, but I think Taryn had something to do with your father's death."

"Tylisha and I think so too, but we can't prove it." Macal replied with disappointment. "After momma died, dad promised Taryn he'd marry her. Three months later they were supposed to get married, but he stood her up at the altar."

"Of course."

"And married her baby sister Claudia the next day."

Macal's last statement caused Thuy to spit out her beer like a gusher. "You gotta be shitting me!"

Jamila

"Nope, dead ass." Macal handed Thuy a napkin to wipe her mouth. "Taryn busted in that wedding wearing her wedding dress. She was so angry it was scary. You can see it in her eyes. I'll never forget those eyes of hate as long as I live. She and Claudia had a bloody fist fight. I think dad wanted to punish Taryn in the worst way for momma's death. He and Claudia took off for their honeymoon, they were found dead in their hotel room. Taryn left town and was never heard from again after the wedding."

"She did it." Macal and Thuy concluded.

The two didn't have any more words left to share and now they couldn't sleep.

Thuy snuggled in Macal's arms and turned on the T.V.

"Look it's Ren and Stimpy!" Thuy cheered like a little kid.

"Fuck yeah. This was my shit." Macal shared Thuy's excitement.

They drunk another beer and sang along to the classics *Happy, Happy, Joy, Joy* and the *Log Song* while watching one of their favorite cartoons from their childhood.

Chapter 3

The morning after Macal woke up feeling refreshed. Thuy was still sleeping comfortably in his arms. He carefully got off the couch to make sure he didn't wake her up. He walked over to the nightstand where his phone was charging and checked his messages. There was one message from Tylisha and over twenty from Lolette. That reminded him of that thing he needed to take care of. First, he checked Tylisha's text message:

Tylisha: Good Morning. We're having breakfast in the dining room.

Macal: See you there!

Then Macal made a phone call from the room phone and patiently waited for an answer. "Front desk."

"Yes, this is Macal Kilborn, I'd like to cancel a reservation."

"What's the reservation number?"

Macal looked through his smartphone to search for the confirmation email. "The number is 802497."

"Alright when do you want the reservation cancelled?"

"Immediately."

"Alright I took care of those changes, the cancellation fee will be added to your bill, along with the accrued charges." The front desk clerk informed.

"That'll be fine, thanks."

"Is there anything else I can help you with today?"

"That'll be all."

"Thanks, enjoy your day."

"You too."

Macal ended the call and looked over at, Thuy, still knocked out on the couch. He walked over to her and woke her up, with a deep strong tongue kiss.

"Good morning beautiful." Macal greeted, Thuy when she woke up.

Kiss good, breath bad, and his ass needs to know it. "Ain't we getting too comfortable? Slobbing me down with your stank ass morning breath?"

Jamila

"Yours don't exactly smell like fresh water, sunrise breeze, or whatever the fuck those smell good shits y'all be using from *Bath and Body Works* and *Victoria's Secret*." Macal shot back.

"And?" Thuy responded like so the fuck what. Macal yanked Thuy off the couch and smacked her hard on the ass. "Oh, so nasty." That shit turned her on.

"I know it." Macal said. "Let's brush these teeth, wash our faces, and join Tylisha and the others for breakfast."

"Good idea." Thuy dug into her overnight bag for her tooth-brush, toothpaste, and face rag.

Macal opened the bathroom door for Thuy and said. "Beautiful queens first."

"Thanks." Thuy giggled and went into the bathroom.

As Macal waited for Thuy to come out, he got a text notification. He had a hunch who it was, and he was right.

Lolette: Nigga, we need to talk!
Macal: Calm your ass down. We will talk later!

Just like that he turned off his phone, without another thought.

****

"Good morning." Macal and Thuy, greeted when they reached Tylisha's table with their plates, taking their seats.

"Morning guys." Everyone at the table greeted back.

"How was the night life?" Thuy asked.

"Fun, I had a great time." Tylisha answered.

"Y'all need to come out with us next time." Enzo suggested.

"Yes, we should." Macal said, noticing someone was missing. "Enzo, where's Amery?"

"I dropped him off at Ligia's momma, Emma's house." Enzo answered. "Amery is gonna spend two days with her and Ligia's stepfather Nico."

"Miss Thuy, what does a sports agent do?" Ayla asked.

Thuy tried her best to explain her occupation. "Let's put it this way. You know how your mom, Enzo and your Uncle Macal, have clients, they do things for?"

22

"Yes." Ayla said.

"I have athletes who are my clients. I represent them when they want a deal, an endorsement, and other things of that nature." Thuy explained. "Example, you know how Amery's stepbrother, Sharmon, is doing those toothpaste commercials?"

"Yes, they're funny." Welton and Ayla laughed.

"I put together the deal to make that happen. Sharmon, is my client. I helped him get that endorsement. You know I represent my cousin Sam I Am? I also helped Y.M. Lewis get that huge NBA contract extension with the New York Knicks." Thuy explained.

"That's cool." Welton and Ayla were in awe.

Out of the blue, Thuy, came up with a fun idea for the kids. "Hey, when we get back home, I'll take you guys along when I do my sports agent rounds. But, only if it's okay with your parents."

"Momma, can we?" Welton and Ayla asked Tylisha.

"Sure, go ahead." Tylisha approved.

"I'm sure Amery would love it, too. But, I'll have to double check with Ligia real quick." Enzo said, then pulled out his phone to send her a quick text.

"What you got going on today?" Macal asked Thuy.

"Today I'm going to a car show. The host is the nephew of a potential client from the New Orleans Pelicans and he invited me. I think I'm winning him over." Thuy stated her itinerary for today. "Would you like to join me if you don't have any plans?"

"Sure, my lady." Macal accepted the invitation.

"Let's get ready."

"Have a nice day guys." Macal and Thuy, bid everybody goodbye, and left the table.

They walked arm and arm out of the dining room, into the elevator. During the short elevator ride, Macal and Thuy, made out like horny teenagers. They didn't want it to end, but it must. The elevator stopped at the second floor and Macal had to get off.

"I'll get ready, then meet you in the lobby." Thuy said.

"Yes ma'am, make sure to wear something sexy." He said with a wink.

"I will sir, make sure to wear something that doesn't make you look all raggedy." Thuy joked, then the elevator door closed.

Macal laughed all the way back to his room. He stopped dead in his tracks when he saw Lolette parked at his door.

"Lolette what the fuck are you still doing here?" He wasn't the least bit amused.

"Why the fuck did you cancel my room. They kicked my ass out of my motherfucking room!" Lolette was heated, but Macal didn't give a fuck. Served her trifling ass right for that shit she pulled last night. Making sure Thuy found her thong in plain sight.

"Because your ass was supposed to be on that fucking plane back to the A!"

"Look you need to..."

"Get the fuck back to Atlanta right now!"

Lolette wasn't going any motherfucking where. She wanted her room and man back. "Nigga you can forget that shit. I ain't leaving, so your lying, dog ass can be all up under that bitch."

Hearing Lolette use the word bitch to describe Thuy, caused something to snap inside Macal. He grabbed Lolette's arm tightly, pulled her towards him hard enough to pull it from its socket and hissed in her face. "Don't you ever fix your fucking mouth to talk about her in that manner again. You understand that shit. Now get the fuck out my face." He slung her out of his path, entered his room, and slammed the door.

Lolette was left completely speechless. The way Macal talked to her and treated her was hard to register in her brain. All she could do was stand there deep in her thoughts, until she heard loud laughter from Tylisha.

"Damn." Tylisha continued to laugh at Lolette's expense. She always thought Lolette was the most pathetic hoe on the planet. She had now officially downgraded her opinion.

"This shit ain't funny." Lolette snapped.

"Yes, the fuck it is." Tylisha kept right on laughing. "Macal brings you here for a fuck and the second Thuy shows up, he kicks you to the curb, leaving you all assed out."

Lolette couldn't stand Tylisha's laughing for another minute, so she stormed off. Lolette could still hear Tylisha's taunting laughter, as she made her way inside the elevator. Once the door closed, Lolette, burst into tears. She thought with Fallon out of the way, Macal, would be all hers. Turns out she couldn't have been more wrong. He didn't choose her. He chose a bitch he's only known for five motherfucking minutes.

Lolette wiped her tears, then started laughing when she re-called Thuy's story, and came up with her own realization. "No wonder that nigga is with her. He loves gullible bitches!"

When the elevator stopped on Lolette's floor, she regained her composure, went to her room to get her bags and prepared to go back home. Yeah this was a huge blow for Lolette, but she'd be alright , because a bitch like her never stayed down for long.

Jamila

Addicted to the Drama 2

Chapter 4

Thuy and Sam, were at Cheddar's having a drink and going over his latest endorsement deal.

"What do you think?" Thuy asked.

"Perfect as usual." Sam answered with satisfaction.

"Awe that means a lot coming from you and that new scent of yours."

Sam raised his eyebrow. "New scent?"

"That Hypnotic Poison perfume." Thuy noted. "When am I gonna meet this new lady of yours?"

Sam had a great feeling about the new woman in his life. He just wasn't sure how everyone else would feel about the pairing. "I'm waiting on the right time. I don't wanna jinx it."

"Gotcha." Thuy nodded with understanding.

"Hi guys." Bryn and Vida, greeted as they approached the table.

Thuy gave her friends a hug and once again smelled a familiar scent on Vida. "Vida maybe I should give you Armani Code instead. You're starting to wear it more than Sam here." She joked.

"Oh, you don't say." Bryn said, glancing at Vida.

"And whoever Sam's new girlfriend is, has the same taste in perfume as you." Thuy said to Vida.

"Really?" Bryn gave Sam a curious look.

"It's time for me to head out." Sam kissed Thuy on the cheek. "Bye baby girl."

"Bye Sam."

"Bye guys." Sam said to Bryn and Vida.

"Bye." Bryn and Vida replied, taking their seats.

"How was New Orleans?" Vida asked Thuy.

"It was great, I closed all the deals, and had fun with Macal and his family." Thuy's phone rung, she looked at the caller I.D. to see who it was. "I gotta take this, be right back."

"Take your time." Bryn said, then Thuy left the table. Once she stepped outside, he blurted out to Vida, like a news reporter. "So Vida how long have you and Sam been fucking?"

Vida was taken aback by Bryn's direct approach at a highly

sensitive private matter. "Nigga is you crazy? Blurting my fucking business out like that. What the fuck is wrong with you?"

"Your point? Now answer the fucking question."

"Me and Sam fucking? Don't be ridiculous. That's absurd. How did you know?" She quickly dropped the act.

"This is Bryn you're talking to."

"You just love showing off that fancy psychiatrist license, don't you?" Vida replied with sarcasm.

"True." Bryn admitted with a cocky smile. "Now how long?"

Somebody had to know sooner or later. Vida thought. "Back in the day I had a little childhood crush on Sam."

"Duh, everybody knew that."

"Can I tell my story?" Vida snapped at Bryn like he was a child.

"Yes ma'am." He answered childlike.

"Good." Vida continued. "Now as I was saying, before I was so rudely interrupted. At Thuy's birthday party Sam and I started talking. We found out we had a lot in common especially with our history of failed relationships, deciding to give up on love and focus on our careers. When Thuy was in the hospital after everything went down with Jeromy, Sam rushed here as fast as he could and stayed at Thuy's house. He was so devastated, that he wasn't there to stop Jeromy. He said he appreciated me for being there for Thuy. We had a few drinks and—it just happened. We were both vulnerable and under the influence."

"I understand that night you two were comforting each other and things went a little too far." Bryn comprehended.

"That's right."

"Okay, so why did you keep giving him the pussy after the fact?"

"Shit that nigga dick was good!" Vida unapologetically answered with glow.

Sam was different, he's a great guy, very handsome. He's tall, sexy, and has a muscular body, covered with smooth deep dark brown skin. Topped off with his thick juicy nine inches she couldn't resist.

"I get it. You two sneaky, nasty, ass freaks are keeping this a secret, because y'all scared of Thuy." Bryn accused.

"We're not scared of her. We just don't know how she's gonna take this." Vida expressed her concern.

"Yeah scared." Bryn reiterated his accusation. "Look you and Sam make each other happy. I've seen the changes in you two. Thuy loves you guys and wants what's best for y'all. Trust me she'll understand and give y'all her blessing. So quit being scary and tell her."

"Shh." Vida shushed Bryn when she saw Thuy coming back. "Who was that?" She asked her.

"Orlando Wall." Thuy answered, taking her seat.

"The talk show host?" Vida asked with amazement.

"Ambrosia gave him his new show last week." Bryn said. "Nice guy. Why did he reach out to you Thuy?"

Thuy sighed and answered. "Good news and bad news. First the good, he wants his new series premiere to feature me."

"That's great!" Vida cheered.

"Congratulations!" Bryn added to the cheering.

"Sounds great doesn't it." Thuy said. "There's one itty bitty, teeny tiny little problem."

"What's the problem?" Vida asked.

"He wants the show to be about the Jeromy thing." Thuy was just putting her life back together. She really didn't want to go through all that shit again, especially in front of a national T.V. audience.

"And you're not ready for that." Bryn read Thuy's mind.

"Hell no." Thuy protested. "But, to be polite I told him I'll think it over."

"Jeromy can't hurt you anymore." Vida said.

"I know." Thuy said. "He's in prison. Looking back on it I got off easy. Unlike women like Onya. You know some people can't believe I have no ill will towards her. What some people don't understand is that Onya was just a victim like I was." She let out a heavy sigh before expressing her latest thought about the interview. "At least I'm still here to tell my side of the story."

"Does this mean you're gonna do the show?" Vida asked.

Jamila

"Let's not get carried away." Thuy didn't say shit about doing the show, but she began to see things in a different perspective. "But I'll truly think about it."

Chapter 5

It's early afternoon, Enzo and Tylisha, were in her bed, cuddling and making out after their third round of lovemaking.

"What a way to spend the day." Enzo said, kissing Tylisha.

"Wasn't it nice of Macal and Thuy, to take the kids for the day so they can shadow Thuy's sports agent duties." Tylisha said with gratitude.

"I need to thank her for giving me the opportunity to spend the day fucking my woman."

"I believe the proper term is, lovemaking." Tylisha corrected sternly.

"Lovemaking—fucking? Let's not ruin the moment with a lot of technical mumbo-jumbo hair splitting." Enzo climbed on top of Tylisha adding. "Unless it's me splitting you in half."

"Uh huh." Tylisha replied, kissing Enzo. "Do we have time to make love, fuck, or whatever you wanna call it, before Macal and Thuy bring the kids back?"

"I think so." Enzo guessed.

"Alright then." Without uttering another word, Tylisha, opened her legs to let Enzo dig deep inside her.

He wiggled his dick inside her pussy making her cum and moan. *Ring—ring—ring!*

"Shit." The sounds of the doorbell pissed Tylisha off, she was about to bust another nut. "Maybe if we ignore them, they'll go away."

"Uh huh!" Enzo went along with Tylisha's obvious futile plan and went back to tearing up the pussy.

The doorbell continued to ring, Tylisha knew it wasn't gonna stop.

She held out until, she got her nut, and said in defeat. "Let me get that." Tylisha kissed Enzo and climbed out the bed.

She threw on some shorts, a tank top, slipped on some flip-flops, and went downstairs to answer the door.

"Who the fuck is this at my door." She mumbled, swinging the door open. When she saw it was Milton her face turned with contempt.

"Tylisha I—" Milton was cut off, with a door slam to the face. He then started banging on the door and yelled. "Tylisha, open this motherfucking door!"

Did this nigga forget that he used to be married to me? Tylisha wondered, who in the fuck Milton was making demands to. Against her character, she opened the door, but only because Enzo was upstairs. "What?" She greeted rudely.

"Where my kids at?"

"They ain't here. Now beat it!"

Tylisha was about to slam the door in Milton's face again, but he caught it, and let himself in the house. "I'll wait then."

"Get the fuck out my house!"

"Not until I see my kids!"

"I told your dumb ass they ain't here. Even if they were, I'm not letting them see your deadbeat, junkie ass!" Tylisha snapped.

"I ain't no junkie!" Milton yelled in defense. "Who told you that bullshit?"

"None of your fucking business." Tylisha answered.

"Baby is there a problem?" Enzo asked with concern making his way downstairs when he heard all the yelling.

Milton saw Enzo, wearing gray sweatpants, no shirt, with his arms around Tylisha in a protective manner. Milton quickly figured he'd interrupted them fucking. "You have got to be fucking kidding me. This the new nigga?" He pointed at Enzo.

"Look your ass need to leave!" Enzo demanded.

Milton rolled up on Enzo, getting in his face. "Nigga you can't tell me what to motherfucking do. Just because you fucking my ex-wife and playing daddy to my kids!" He spewed out with hate.

He took a swing at Enzo, but he ducked under it, then Enzo punched Milton in his jaw. The men tussled and started throwing punches.

"Please stop!" Tylisha yelled in terror. "Please stop!"

Milton punched Enzo in his chest, Enzo punched Milton in the eye. Tylisha pulled Enzo off of Milton. She wanted the fighting to stop, she didn't want the chance of the kids walking in on this.

Addicted to the Drama 2

Worst case scenario Macal, might join Enzo and beat Milton's ass.

Tylisha pulled Enzo on the couch and tended to his wounds with care.

Milton couldn't stand seeing them together like that and gave up. "Fuck this shit." He said, then stormed out of the house.

Tylisha shook her head, closed, and locked the door. "I should've told you Milton was back before our trip." She apologized, joining Enzo back on the couch. "His pop up threw me for a loop."

"I understand baby." Enzo rubbed Tylisha's cheek.

"It's a good thing I have a man that can fight." Tylisha said, they laughed. "I don't know what I'm gonna do about him wanting to see the kids."

"I know it's a lot to think about." Enzo said. "Just know that whatever decision you make, I'll stand by you and the kids."

"Thanks baby." Tylisha kissed Enzo. "Since you're probably sore from the fight, I guess you won't be able to make love, fuck or whatever you wanna call it, huh?"

"Tylisha, Milton punched me in my face and chest. Not my dick and ball sack." Enzo implied.

Tylisha caught the hint and dashed back upstairs giggling, with Enzo on her tail. They hopped back in bed to finish their fourth round of lovemaking.

Meanwhile, Milton sat in his gold Bentley, snorting up his last bit of cocaine, then pulled out the driveway headed back to his condo.

33

Jamila

Addicted to the Drama 2

Chapter 6

Welton, Ayla, and Amery enjoyed Thuy's special treat. They had a great time watching the *Atlanta Falcons* and the *Atlanta Hawks*, practice and being introduced to the players. One of the players from the Atlanta Hawks, invited them to his daughter's sixth birthday party at Chuck E. Cheese's. Amery volunteered to sing Happy Birthday to her. The kids were playing in the ball-pit, while Macal and Thuy, played Dance-Dance Revolution. Thuy ended up falling flat on her ass, Macal busted out laughing at her expense.

"Boy quit laughing and help me up!" Thuy yelled.

"Okay—okay." Macal tried to cease the laughter, as he helped Thuy up. "Our pizza should be ready now."

"You should be ashamed of yourself." Thuy playfully scolded, Macal, as they walked to the counter to get their pizza. "Laughing at me like that, I could've broken my ass!"

Macal zoomed in on Thuy's way too much junk in the trunk and replied. "Trust me baby, you ain't got shit to worry about."

"Not in front of the kids, Amery is old enough to know what you talking about."

"You're right. We don't need Enzo, Ligia, and Tylisha cussing us out." Macal said, as they sat at their table.

"I think the kids enjoyed themselves today." Thuy took a bite out of her pizza. I know, I did."

"Me too." Macal's phone started ringing, he rolled his eyes with annoyance. "Who the fuck is this?" He pulled out his phone and saw it was Lolette. He pressed ignore, putting the phone on silent.

"Who was that?"

"Nobody important." Macal answered, shoving the phone back into his pocket. "Now back to you. Have I told you what an amazing, beautiful, unique woman you are?"

"Um—not within the past hour, no." Thuy answered with sarcasm.

"Okay, well you are an amazing, beautiful, unique woman."

"Thanks, you sexy, smooth, tasty tall glass of chocolate milk you." Thuy complimented smiling.

Jamila

That shit was corny as fuck! Macal thought. "Chocolate milk, Thuy, really?" He gave her a crazy look.

"Well nigga I tried. We all can't be experts at flattering like you."

"You silly, silly girl." Macal chuckled and Thuy joined in.

"Orlando Wall called me again this morning." Thuy volunteered.

"Orlando Wall? He's huge, Grandma Doris and her friend Gladys can't wait for his show to come back on." Macal said.

"He wants me to be featured in his new series premiere."

"Baby that's great."

"He wants to talk about the Jeromy thing."

"I think you should go for it."

"Really?"

Macal held Thuy's hand, looking into her eyes, with tenderness and care. "Baby you survived a traumatic ordeal. People wanna see you. Hear you tell your story. They're a lot of people who has been through some serious shit. You can inspire them. Just like Christina Crawford."

"Inspire people—me?" Thuy was unsure about this.

"Yes. Some people don't even make it out alive to tell their side of the story. Just think about it."

"You're making me sound like a superhero." Thuy joked.

"Does that mean I get to see you in a tight, sexy, ass superhero costume?" Macal teased, and Thuy pulled his leg from under the table. "Girl you strong. What the hell am I gonna do with you?"

"Love me." Thuy flashed her glowing, charming smile.

"That can be arranged." Macal leaned in and gave Thuy a quick PG-13 kiss, that was appropriate for a restaurant full of kids. "When was the last time you talked to your dad and siblings?"

"I'm supposed to meet with Tori and Jett later on this week." Thuy sighed. "Daddy's birthday is coming up, they want the three of us to plan something together. In other words, Tori and Jett, plan it and I pay for it."

"They're actually including you in something?" Macal was stunned. From what Thuy told him Jett and Tori couldn't stomach being in the same room with her.

"Yep. I don't know what to think. I don't put anything past them. After all they are their momma's kids." Thuy expressed her suspicions.

"Maybe they wanna call a truce." Macal tried to be optimistic.

Thuy laughed out loud. "Macal you are a fucking riot. That shit was hilarious." She looked up, saw the serious look on his face, and tried to change her tune. "Oh, poor baby, you were actually serious." She said to Macal, in a voice like she was talking to a toddler, then pinched his cheek.

"I know they did some fucked up shit in the past. But, you'll never know what they're up to until you meet with them." Macal said.

"I feel you." Thuy nodded.

"You know what they say. Kill them with kindness."

I like the sound of that! "Alright Macal you've convinced me. I'll meet with Tori and Jett. I'll also call Orlando to say yes to the interview. Damn boy, you're having a huge effect on me."

"I do? Wow and I didn't even tear the pussy up yet?"

Thuy pulled Macal's leg from under the table again. "Quit being nasty in front of these kids."

"Baby if you want nasty, all you gotta do is ask." Macal winked.

"Oh—la—la. My thong is getting wet." Thuy mumbled under her breath, but intentionally loud enough for Macal to hear her.

That remark made Macal's dick super stiff. "Now who's being nasty?" They laughed.

Jamila

Chapter 7

"Tylisha my dear." Vax greeted Tylisha, letting her in the house.

"Hey Vax." Tylisha greeted back. "Hi Amery."

"Hi Tylisha." Amery greeted, hugging Tylisha.

"I'm about to take Amery to school and head to the office. Thanks for looking after Ligia for me. She's a little under the weather today." Vax said with gratitude.

"Anytime, Vax. You guys have a nice day." Vax and Amery, left, then Tylisha made her way upstairs, into Vax and Ligia's bedroom.

"Ligia." Tylisha called out. She heard something coming from the bathroom. She slowly opened the door, horrified at the scene she walked in on. "Ligia!"

Ligia was slumped over the toilet, her mouth was covered with bloody vomit. "Is Vax and Amery gone?" She asked with fright.

"They just left." Tylisha rushed to Ligia's aid, helping her off the floor.

She helped Ligia get in bed, then went inside the closet to get some towels. She wet one of the towels to clean Ligia up. Then she cleaned the bathroom and put the towels in the laundry room.

When Tylisha returned to her bedside, Ligia asked. "Why are you here?"

"Vax called me. He wanted me to look after you today, because you were under the weather." Tylisha answered.

"Yeah I have a headache." Ligia was half truthful.

"Ligia, this is more than a headache." Tylisha knew exactly what was going on, because Gladys had the exact same problem. She and Doris took care of her. "Vax doesn't know you have cancer, does he?"

"I don't know what you're taking about." Ligia denied.

"Girl, I know what blood in vomit means. My grandmomma's best friend had this same problem, when I was in high school. You might as well fess up." Tylisha said.

Shit. Somebody was gonna know sooner or later! Ligia didn't really want anyone to know about this. "Ovarian cancer." Ligia confessed. "I was diagnosed two months after Vax and I came back from our honeymoon. I went into remission a year after, but now it's starting to come back."

"Who all knows about this?"

"Until now—no one."

"What? You've been going through this shit alone for almost three motherfucking years. You haven't told a soul? Not even your momma or your own husband?" Tylisha couldn't imagine keeping anything like this inside.

"Tylisha I don't want to worry, or be a burden to anybody, okay."

"What are you talking about? They need to know."

Ligia shook her head with tears in her eyes. "Momma already lost Sasha. She can't handle the possibility of losing me, too. Her only living child. It took everything for Vax to give love another chance after Lily. I can't do that to him. I just can't."

"And holding it in is not helping anybody either. It's definitely not helping you. Trust me, your family would want to be there to support you." This woman needed someone to lean on during her serious crisis. Obviously Tylisha had to be that person. "Until you come to your senses and tell your loved ones, know that you no longer have to go through this alone." She pulled Ligia in her arms, kissing her forehead.

"Thanks, Tylisha." Ligia wiped her tears and climbed out of bed. "Let me get pretty for this doctor's appointment. See you later."

Did she just tell me see you later? "That's a funny thing to say to the person who's driving you to your doctor's appointment."

"You're actually gonna take me to my appointment?" Ligia asked with disbelief.

"What part of you're not going through this alone did your ass not understand?"

"Okay—okay! Of course, you know this is gonna be between us, right?" Ligia asked for confirmation.

"Of course." Tylisha agreed.

"You know that also means you can't tell Enzo either, right?"

"I know."

"I mean it Tylisha. Don't tell him. I know his dick game is off the chain. But, don't let him break you!" Tylisha gave Ligia a crazy look. Hearing another woman describe her man's dick made her feel some type of way. "Don't look at me like that. You know I was married to the nigga for six years, Amery didn't just fall out the sky." Ligia implied. She remembered how amazing Enzo was in bed. That nigga's dick would make a bitch confess to shit she didn't even do. Actually sex was the only reason their marriage lasted as long as it did. Ligia needed to make sure Tylisha wasn't dick-matized enough to blurt out her health problems to her best friend/ex-husband. Ligia couldn't take the chance of him running his mouth to her momma and their son.

"Right—right! Now get your ass in that shower. Go brush your teeth, gargle, fix your hair and makeup all nice and pretty. We need to get to this doctor's appointment on time. I'll go ahead and get your outfit ready for you." Tylisha ordered, like she was Ligia's momma.

"Enzo and Macal were right. You are bossy and demanding." Ligia replied.

Tylisha pointed to the bathroom door and ordered again in a more serious tone. "Bitch, get in that fucking bathroom!"

"Yes ma'am." Ligia playfully obeyed, walking into the bathroom.

"Let's see Welton, Ayla, Amery, Enzo, Macal, now this makes six kids." Tylisha sighed.

Ligia swung opened the door wearing a shower cap and nothing else. "Then that'll make Amery your grandbaby." She teased.

Tylisha rose out of her seat, positioned her hand like she was about to pimpslap the hell out of Ligia. "Hoe you better—"

Ligia giggled and went back in the bathroom.

Tylisha plumped back on the bed and joined in on Ligia's giggling. *Nice body—no homo!*

Jamila

Chapter 8

Thuy was on her way to meet with Jett and Tori, at a bar and grill, she needed to mentally and emotionally prepare herself. The only person who could help her with that was her mother. Thuy approached the front door, rang the doorbell, and to her surprise it took longer than usual to get an answer.

"Baby." Isla greeted, Thuy, with a hug and kiss on the cheek.

"Momma." Thuy greeted back, entering the house. Then the ladies took their seats on the couch.

Greg walked down the stairs and kissed Isla. "I'll be back."

"Take your time." Isla said.

Greg hugged Thuy. "Hey baby girl!"

"Hey." Thuy said with a smile. When Greg took his leave, Thuy turned to Isla. "It took you a while to answer the door."

"Sorry Thuy, I was a little preoccupied."

"With what?"

Isla blushed, "Well—uh—"

"Noted." Thuy figured it out. She was happy that her mother was happy, but Thuy didn't need to hear the details about her mother and stepfather's sexcapades. "I'm here because, I need a pep talk."

"Why?"

"After I leave here, I'm meeting with Tori and Jett, I need to prepare myself." Thuy sighed.

"In other words, you're hoping for the best, but expecting the worst?" Isla guessed.

"How do you know me so well?" It was like Isla read Thuy's mind.

"All part of my motherly duties."

"Macal said I should kill them with kindness."

"Sounds like a good idea to me." Isla agreed. "Hopefully for their sakes they changed their attitudes. I blame their mother for their behavior."

"So, do I."

"Finding out your daddy was married was the most humiliating, heart-breaking moment of my life."

Jamila

Isla was deeply in love with Olson. When she found out she was pregnant with Thuy. Olson proposed to her, promising her a beautiful life and family. How in the fuck was he supposed to give Isla those things when he already had a wife and kids, he neglected telling her about?

After Isla had Thuy, in the delivery room, she and Olson were filled with pride and joy with their beautiful bundle of joy. The moment was interrupted by Mycha, barging in with Jett and Tori in tow, all hell broke loose. She was all outraged, causing a scene exposing everything.

Isla told Mycha, she didn't know Olson was married. Mycha called Isla a liar and slapped her hard across the face, not giving a fuck about almost knocking Thuy out of her arms. As far as Mycha was concerned, Thuy should've never been born, and didn't deserve any type of respect. Isla gave the nearest nurse the baby, jumped out of the hospital bed, and beat Mycha's ass.

At the end Isla broke up with Olson, forcing him to pay child support to face his responsibilities. Isla knew Mycha, was a victim of Olson's deception. However, that didn't excuse her cruelty towards her little girl, who was completely innocent in this complicated bullshit. Isla told Mycha the truth, she apologized once, and if she wanted to remain a bitter hateful bitch, that was her motherfucking problem. Nobody told her ass to stay with her trifling husband once the truth came out.

"What do you think I should do?" Thuy asked.

"I know how much you want them to accept you and the kind of person you are. What I suggest you do, is use your best judgment, and take baby steps." Isla gave Thuy the best advice she could.

"Yes momma." Thuy nodded. "I'm gonna do that interview." She added.

"That's good baby." Isla hugged Thuy. "What changed your mind? The last time we talked about it, you were dead set against it."

"Macal made me see the whole thing in a different light. He said telling my story might help others." Thuy explained.

"He makes a good point. I see this Macal, boy is having an

effect on you." Isla pointed out.

"Yes, he is." Thuy smiled at the mention of Macal's name. "We're having a lot of fun together and he's great to talk to."

"I spoke with his grandmother yesterday. She's such a sweet woman."

"And have you seen Macal, with his sister and her kids? He really loves them." Thuy said. "Only crazy thing is, his momma died on my birthday."

"That's freaky!"

"He and his mom were very close. He was thirteen and Tylisha was seven. Their dad died about three or four months afterwards." Thuy said.

"Those poor babies." Isla said with sympathy. "I know Doris did her best. I don't know how she did it."

Isla's heart went out to Doris, for losing her only child, and raising her grandbabies by herself. Not too long ago, Isla was almost in her shoes. She didn't know what she would've done if that hateful bastard Jeromy's plan worked. She could've lost her little girl. The thought of what could've happened, caused Isla to pull Thuy into her arms tightly, not wanting to let her go.

"I love you, baby girl." Isla said with deep love in her heart.

Thuy had a pretty good idea why the hug was a bit more intense. She guessed Isla thought about what Jeromy did and the possible outcome. Thuy was thankful to be alive, but she wished she had Day'zon with her. Not a day went by that Thuy didn't wish her little boy was in her arms. It wasn't easy, but Thuy managed to break the protective embrace.

"I love you too, momma." Thuy said getting ready to leave. "I better get going, wish me luck."

"Good luck baby."

Jamila

Addicted to the Drama 2

Chapter 9

Tori was sitting at a table, at a bar and grill, waiting on Jett and Thuy to show up. She saw Jett walking towards the table with one of his typical gold-digging hoodrats on his arm.

"Hey, baby girl." Jett hugged his little sister.

"Hi Jett." Tori cheerfully greeted. She turned to the hoodrat and greeted dryly. "Iesha."

"It's Monique." She rudely corrected.

"Oh, my bad. It's hard to keep all of y'all straight." Tori snickered on the sly.

"Whatever." Monique rolled her eyes.

"Is she coming?" Jett asked as everyone took their seats.

"Yeah, she called and said she was on the way. She had to stop by her momma's house first." Tori informed.

"She need to hurry her ass up." Monique said.

Who the fuck do this bitch think she is? Tori thought of Monique. She saw Thuy coming their way, "Here she comes now."

Thuy kept it basic, wearing black jeans, a white form-fitting polo shirt, bright white Nike's and a black and white polka dotted designer handbag. She made her way towards her half siblings and Jett's ratchet ghetto companion, dressed from head to toe in obvious knock offs.

"Hello, my beloved elder siblings." Thuy made herself known. "How are you guys doing today?"

"Great." Jett and Tori replied.

Thuy took her seat and broke the ice, by asking. "What's new?"

"The kids are doing great in school." Tori said.

"How are Alicia, A.J. and Clarke?" Thuy asked.

"Good." Tori didn't think Thuy even knew her kid's names. "You actually remember their names?"

"Of course." Thuy actually loved her niece and nephews and they were crazy about her. They're great kids. Obviously, they took after their fathers. "See how it feels having a sibling that cares about the goings on in your life, must be nice." She said with sarcasm.

"Here we go with this bullshit again." Tori rolled her eyes.

Jamila

Thuy looked at Tori up and down, adding something else. "Oh, I'm doing fine after my little ordeal that was all over the news. Thanks for asking."

"Glad to hear it." Tori said.

"It would've been nice if y'all came to the hospital to see me, but I understand. After all, I'm just an outside kid. Who gives a fuck what happens to me?" Thuy said with slight contempt.

"Like your ass wanted us there."

"Because, I know y'all don't give a fuck!"

"If that was true they would've never invited your stuck up bitter bitch ass up in here!" Monique threw in her unwanted two cents.

"Hi Jett." Thuy ignored Monique and greeted.

"Thuy." Jett responded.

"Thuy, that's sweet." Thuy said. "It was only yesterday, your lecherous, disgusting, friends nicknamed me, Thuy No-Close. I wonder where they got that from."

"Bitch get the fuck over that shit and run that motherfucking money." Monique snapped at Thuy.

Of course! Thuy rolled her eyes. "How much y'all need?"

Tori was getting super close to slapping the taste out of the bitch's mouth, but now was not the time. She needed to get this money from Thuy and if Monique fucked it up, she was gonna stomp that hoe. "You know daddy's birthday coming up." Tori reminded Thuy.

"I'm aware of y'all daddy, slash my sperm donor's birthday." Thuy said.

"Anyway, daddy wants to celebrate with his kids." Tori said.

"I'm included in this celebration?" Thuy asked with disbelief. "I know y'all don't include me in shit."

"We need the money."

"For what?"

"None of your motherfucking business!" Monique demanded.

Tori rolled her eyes at Monique and continued. "Look Thuy—"

"Hold on for a second, Tori." Thuy turned facing Monique. She had to put an end to this hoe's shit, she decided to take a different approach, rather than knocking her the fuck out. "Who the fuck are you supposed to be darling?"

Monique, was offended by the question. "I'm Jett's woman."

Thuy chuckled. "My dear girl, just because my brother is sharing his community dick with you. Or dressing you up in the finest knock offs. That doesn't make you relevant enough to blurt out your selfish, dumb, ghetto ass input in our family matters."

"Exactly." Tori agreed which surprised Jett and Thuy.

"This coming from the dumb bitch, who didn't know she was friends with one of her man's hoes!" Monique hit below the belt.

"She's so lucky we're in public." Tori whispered to Thuy.

"You know." Thuy agreed and went back to Monique. "Darling, will you please shut your ignorant ass up? So, me and my siblings can continue our discussion about our father's birthday, and the money I might give them?"

"Might? Your ass better motherfucking do it!" Monique ordered.

On that note, Thuy decided to take her leave before she'd have to resort to tearing a bitch's head off. "I'll call you later, we'll talk more. Good day." She bid her siblings goodbye.

As Thuy walked off, she heard Monique say. "And your ass better hurry the fuck up."

Thuy turned around and walked over to Monique. "Knock—knock."

Monique rolled her eyes and asked. "Who's there?"

"This." Thuy pulled hard on a long loose thread from Monique's fake Gucci bag, causing the whole bag to unravel, and break apart. The contents of the cheap inimitable handbag fell all over the floor causing onlookers to turn their heads, laughing.

"Shit!" Monique shrieked in embarrassment. "Jet what the fuck did you buy me?"

"Baby—I—" Jett struggled to come up with a lie.

"Nigga, you ain't shit!"

Thuy smirked in victory, strutting out the door. She entered her car and got a text notification from Tori.

Jamila

Tori: Way to go Thuy, you a bad bitch!

Thuy giggled. She couldn't believe after all these years she and Tori, finally found something in common. They both didn't like Jett's taste in women. What an icebreaker.

Thuy sent a reply: *Thanks, what you doing later?*
Tori: Nothing.
Thuy: Wanna meet me at the Platinum Palace, around eight for drinks?
Tori: I'm there!

Chapter 10

"Fallon, loved the cake you baked for her last week. She really ap-preciated it." Naomi told Doris over the phone.

"How's she doing?" Doris asked with concern.

"She's doing okay." Naomi answered. "She's still not approved for sign in and out."

"Don't worry, she will."

"How's the family?"

"Great."

"How's Macal?"

"He's doing okay for the most part." Doris tried to answer as honestly as she could. "He's dating Thuy. The girl that baseball player tried to have killed."

"The fuck nigga!" Naomi hissed. "That girl is so brave. I'm gonna watch her interview when it comes on. I hope Macal get his shit together for both their sakes and that hoe Lolette, is gone for good!"

"Amen."

"There's something else about that, Thuy, girl. I don't know what it is. But, she reminds me of someone. I just can't put my fin-ger on it." Then Naomi got serious. "If I haven't said it enough lately, thank you and Tylisha, for being there for Fallon during her time of need."

"Fallon is a sweet girl, glad to help." Doris was interrupted by a knock at the door. "Someone's at the door. I'll talk to you later, bye."

"Bye."

The call ended, Doris answered the door. "Tylisha baby, what a surprise!" Doris greeted, letting her granddaughter in the house.

"Hey, Grandma Doris. I know I should've called first, but I need to talk to you." Tylisha sounded distressed, taking a seat on the couch.

"What's wrong, baby?"

"It's Milton, he's back."

"Milton!" Doris never thought she'd ever hear that name again.

Jamila

"That little nigga is back?"

"He wants to see the kids." Tylisha sighed. "He's been bothering me about it night and day."

"What did you tell him?"

"I told him no. I'm not putting the babies through that drama."

"You need to put those babies first." Doris understood Tylisha's decision. "If his ass wanna reenter their lives, he has to understand, he has a lot of work to do first."

"That's what I tried to tell him, but he won't listen."

"You gotta make him listen, with just honest, no bullshit talk." Doris then thought of something very important. "Let me ask you this. Do you want Milton in the babies' lives?"

Tylisha was still pissed at Milton, but she couldn't ignore the fact, he was Welton and Ayla's father. "He has the right to see them of course, but he just can't pop up like nothing happened."

"Good point." Doris agreed. "Also, you need to forgive and let go of any hostility you have towards Milton before you bring the kids into this."

"Forgiveness is tough." Tylisha was feeling what Doris was saying, but that shit seemed impossible.

"Baby nobody said forgiveness was easy. Forgiveness is for you, not them. You're a sweet girl. Don't let a nigga's foolish actions poison you. That's where the forgiveness comes in." Doris explained.

"What you're saying is, I should work on forgiving Milton first? So, I'll be able to talk to him about the kids in a rational, reasonable manner, without anger." Tylisha comprehended like a student in class.

"Now you're getting it!" Doris congratulated like a teacher, proud of her brilliant pupil.

Tylisha flashed back to a conversation, she and Doris had about her grandfather. She wondered how Doris managed to forgive a man, that promised to love and cherish her. Who instead, caused her nothing but, heartache and pain until the day he died.

"How did you forgive daddy and granddaddy?" Tylisha asked.

Doris went on to answer. "Your granddaddy, I loved him

52

unconditionally. I hated what he put me through, but he didn't deserve to die like that. If I hadn't forgiven him, I would've let that anger buildup inside me, and ended up being one of those mean, nasty old ladies, that little kids are scared of."

"I feel you." That made perfect sense to Tylisha. When she was a kid, she thought those types of elderly people just loved being evil and nasty to everyone, especially kids. Now she realized they were like that for a reason.

"Plus, your momma had something to do with it too, and later you, Macal, and the babies." Doris added.

"What made you forgive daddy?"

"Forgiving him was a lot easier." Doris said. "After his funeral, I learned some things about your daddy, that helped me understand him better."

"What did you learn about him?"

"Your momma already knew this. That explained why she gave him so many chances. That pure heart of hers." Doris said. "Your Aunt Ruby on your daddy's side, told me about Rufus' childhood."

"What did she tell you?"

"Turns out Rufus and Thuy have something in common when it comes to fathers."

Tylisha flashed back to one of her conversations with Thuy about her childhood and remembered what she said about her father. "Daddy was an outside kid?" She guessed.

"Yes, he was." Doris confirmed. "His daddy was a married pastor. He saw Rufus and the rest of his outside kids in secret. They couldn't speak to him in public, call him, or anything. In case you are wondering. Yes, he was still fucking his baby mommas. Ruby said Rufus grew to despise his parents."

"I can see that." Tylisha empathized.

How could Rufus respect a father, who treated him like a shameful secret. A mother who entertained his bullshit and didn't respect herself enough to keep her legs closed? She even allowed her children to be neglected by him.

"Things got so bad Rufus moved in with Ruby when he was thirteen." Doris said. "His daddy died when Macal was about to turn three. Rufus couldn't even go to the funeral."

Tylisha shook her head. How could her father, know how to love her mother, the right way? He didn't exactly have the best examples of a normal relationship growing up.

"You're a good woman, Grandma Doris." Tylisha hugged Doris.

"Thanks. You're not so bad yourself. I think I did a pretty decent job." Doris bragged with pride.

Doris and Tylisha laughed.

Addicted to the Drama 2

Chapter 11

Thirteen-year-old Macal, was sitting on his bed with the T.V. on, while the rest of the family was downstairs. He reached under the bed, pulled out a Playboy Magazine, and his Vaseline ready to jack off. He heard his bedroom door open and close, causing him to drop the magazine, and Vaseline jar on the floor. He looked up, there stood Taryn. His father's main mistress and his mother's worst enemy. She was standing before him, wearing a baby blue and white sexy see-through nightie.

"Taryn, what the fuck are you doing here?" Macal realized something wasn't right about this scene. "Wait a minute, how the fuck did you make it upstairs? Everybody's in the living room."

"I wanted to see you."

"Why?"

"What do you mean why? I saw the way you were looking at me." Taryn strutted towards Macal, in all her lustful sexiness.

Macal tried to play it off. He stood on his feet, trying to suppress his forbidden desires. "I don't know what the he—"

"Shhh." Taryn gently placed her index finger over Macal's lips. "Baby don't front, I saw you peeking in the room, watching me getting fucked."

'Busted.' Macal thought. "Look—"

"Shhh, I know you liked what you saw. Do you know why my pussy was so wet?" Taryn asked.

"Why?" Macal didn't know why he'd even asked that question. He'd basically just confirmed she was right. Taryn's half-naked body, was making it hard for him to think logically.

"Watching you stroke your dick turned me the fuck on." Taryn confessed. She looked on the floor at the Playboy Magazine and Vaseline jar. "You men would rather jack off to naked bitches in pictures and videos, then fuck a real woman standing right in front of you." She giggled.

"But—"

"Shhh." Taryn shut Macal up with a kiss. "You're just a baby, so you're excused." She reached into Macal's sweatpants, pulling

55

out his dick and was impressed by its size. "A baby with a grown man's dick, like father, like son I see."

Macal tried to snap out of it and gain control over this crazy ass situation. "Look, you need to get your ass outta here right motherfuckin—"

Taryn took off her thong, stuffing it in Macal's mouth. "Sorry, but you need to shut the fuck up." Macal couldn't do nothing, but suck on Taryn's tasty pussy juices through her thong. "Taste good doesn't it?"

Macal nodded for his answer.

Taryn got on her knees and yanked Macal's pants down. She took Macal's dick, jammed it in her mouth, and sucked hard on his dick. Macal, took the thong out of his mouth, threw it on the floor, and let out a soft moan. Feeling Taryn's warm wet mouth, covering his dick was too much for him to handle, causing him to immediately release his cum deep inside Taryn's mouth. She swallowed every drop.

"You taste good yourself." Taryn said, smiling. Macal, helped her off the floor. "Now you need to learn how to not be a two-minute nigga."

Taryn slipped out of her nightie, Macal's mouth hung wide open. "Shit, you sexy as fuck."

"Thanks cutie." Taryn blushed.

Macal laid Taryn, flat on the bed, and spread opened her legs. He stuck his head between her legs, using his tongue, to lick all over her pussy. He licked all over her lips, fold, and clit. He loved the taste of Taryn's juices. It tasted like red Kool-Aid. He licked every trace of juice he could, then lifted his head to see the look of sexual satisfaction on Taryn's face.

"I see you can eat pussy." Taryn took a deep breath, as Macal started undressing. "Very well I may add."

Macal pulled Taryn into a surprise lip-lock, "Now who's talking too fucking much? Now get ready to be fucked!" He commanded.

Young Macal's boldness turned Taryn on, "Okay."

Macal climbed on top of Taryn, grabbing a handful of ass

underneath. "Girl, where did you get all this ass and titties?"

Taryn giggled, admiring this young boy's sexy body and braced herself for whatever fuck he could dish out. "Since you have a grown man's dick. Let's see if you can fuck like one." She dared.

"Baby you ain't said nothing, but a word." Macal inserted his dick inside Taryn's hot steamy center.

Her pussy was wet and tight, Macal, was filled with excitement, from how she made his dick feel. He started beating the pussy up like it owed him money.

"Oh shit!" Taryn screamed with pleasure. "Ah, oh fuck!"

"Shit, this is so good!" Macal grunted. "I'm loving this pussy, baby."

"Oh baby!" Taryn moaned. "Oh baby, you the best."

"What was that shit you was talking about me needing to fuck like a grown ass man?"

"Baby, you fuck better than a grown ass man!"

Macal was giving the pussy some more aggressive punishment, when he heard his dad's voice yell. "What the fuck is going on here?"

Macal and Taryn, turned and saw Rufus' face of anger, along with Belinda's face of shock, staring at them. Macal didn't know what to say, he was frozen, but Taryn wasn't fazed. As far as, she was concerned if Rufus was gonna stay married to Belinda. She was free to fuck whoever she wanted. Who better to take his place, then his son? That'll teach that bastard to trick her into aborting their baby. She thought.

"Nothing, just getting fucked by a real man, with some great dick. Not a nigga whose dick is all shriveled, worn out, and used up." Taryn insulted, placing her attention back to her new hot young lover. "Where were we, baby?"

"We were right here, baby." Macal quickly reentered Taryn, hitting her spot just right, making her bust a fat nut. "Aahhh!"

Taryn's moan of pleasure, caused Rufus to roll up on them. He pushed Macal out of the way, then slapped Taryn, hard across the face. "Nasty, filthy bitch!"

Rufus began to savagely beat Taryn. Yes, he was married to somebody else, but watching his mistress giving the pussy to another man, fucked up his ego. To make it worse, that man was his very own son, and she was enjoying it.

"Dad, let her go!" Macal tried to stop Rufus, from beating the shit out of Taryn, but Belinda held him back for protection.

"Taryn, I'm sorry—baby I'm sorry!"

****

"Nigga, wake your ass up!" Lolette woke Macal, up from his dream fantasy about Taryn.

He'd been having those same disturbing dreams regularly since his mother died.

Macal yawned, "Lolette, what?"

"Your ass fell asleep, I wanna fuck again." Lolette said.

"Well get to sucking." Macal ordered.

Lolette placed her head on his lap, taking him into her mouth. She was only able to give the dick three sucks, before Macal realized it was almost six-o'clock.

"Oh shit, it's six-o'clock." Macal moved Lolette's head out of the way, grabbed the remote control from the nightstand, and turned on the T.V.

"What the fuck?" Lolette complained, as Macal turned the channel to the Orlando Wall Show.

Orlando was a tall, slender, light-skinned man in his late forties, with a bald head, and a full jet-black beard. He went on to introduce the show.

"Good evening everybody. I'm Orlando Wall, welcome to the premiere of my brand-new show. I have with me right now, the all-around beautiful, Thuy Ellis. She's one of the best sports agents in the country and the owner of Thuy's Audis dealership. Thuy, thanks for coming."

"Thanks for having me, Orlando." Thuy greeted. "After all the begging and pleading you did, not to mention blowing up my phone. I finally decided to drop by." She joked, with a charming laugh.

Orlando and the audience joined in.

"Isn't she something?" Orlando rhetorically asked the audience.

"Awe you're too kind." Thuy said to Orlando.

"Now, Thuy we're here to get your side of the story involving the Jeromy Fuller case." Orlando explained.

"Anytime." Thuy sighed, then began telling her story. "I guess the best place to start, is the beginning. Jeromy was my boyfriend, who later became my fiancé. In the beginning things were good. Then it all went downhill—"

"The fucking bitch!" Lolette hissed under her breath.

"What, was that?" Macal asked.

"I sneezed." Lolette lied.

"Oh, bless you." Without another thought Macal placed his attention back on the show.

"Now, tell us about that night." Orlando said.

Thuy froze for a moment. She didn't know how she was gonna tell this part of the story.

"Thuy, are you okay?" Orlando asked with concern.

Thuy snapped back to reality, she decided to let her heart do the talking. "Not really, but I gotta put on my big girl panties and tell it. Through it all, I'm still standing. I knew coming here to tell my story wasn't gonna be easy. But, my story needs to be told. To show all women, that we're survivors. We all have a story to tell. Our stories need to be told, in order to teach young ladies in this generation, and the next, that they can rise above and overcome."

The studio audience, including Orlando gave a standing ovation. Thuy's words hit close to home.

"I love you, Thuy." Macal said with admiration and passion, pissing off Lolette even more, intensifying her hatred for Thuy.

Thuy went on to talk about that night. "Jeromy and I, hopped into his chrome Porsche headed to his cabin. We were traveling down Fuller Road. Everything was cool until the strangest thing happened. A speeding black limo, flew past almost knocking us off the road."

"What the—" Macal pressed rewind on the remote to make sure he heard, Thuy, right and pressed play.

"We were traveling down Fuller Road. Everything was cool

Jamila

until the strangest thing happened. A speeding black limo, flew past almost knocking us off the road. Jeromy and I, couldn't believe it. Then we saw a van—"

"Thuy and Jeromy, were in that car from the night of the accident." Macal concluded.

Macal's past bitch, almost killed his future bitch. Interesting. Lolette thought, cracking a smile. She snuggled in Macal's arms, paying close attention to the show, quietly taking accurate notes, that could be of possible use to her in the future.

Addicted to the Drama 2

Chapter 12

Doing the interview was difficult, but Thuy, managed to make it through. It felt great getting all of that shit off her chest. Now she was on her way to The Cheesecake Factory, to celebrate Olson's birthday. That night out with Tori, went surprisingly well. They had a good time, Thuy, was more open to idea of burying the hatchet.

Thuy, walked into the restaurant, and found the reserved table.

Olson jumped up, pulling Thuy into a big hug. "Baby girl, you made it!"

"Happy birthday, daddy!" Thuy kissed Olson on the cheek. "Hi, Tori, hi Jett!"

"I'm glad you're here." Jett admitted, hugging Thuy.

"Girl, you look beautiful." Tori complimented, hugging Thuy.

"Thanks, so do you." Tori replied.

"Hey, what about me? I ain't ugly." Jett joked.

"You alright." Tori and Thuy, laughed.

"Don't worry daddy. We told the staff not to sing Happy Birth-day." Tori said.

"Good." Olson said, relieved. "What's new with everybody?" Olson asked as everyone took their seats.

"Monique and I, broke up." Jett shared.

"Good!" Thuy and Tori responded in unison.

"She was nothing, but a tacky, gold-digging hoe anyway." Thuy insulted.

"Tell me about it, good looking out." Jett and Thuy, bumped fists.

"Anytime."

The waitress came to take their orders. Everyone looked at their menus that were placed on the table deciding what to order. The trio decided to get the exact same thing, which was shrimp scampi, lob-ster, and steak. The waitress jotted down their orders and took her leave. Thuy, pulled Olson's birthday cake out, from under the table, and set up the candles so he could blow them out and make his birthday wish.

"Daddy, did you make a birthday wish?" Thuy asked.

"It's already been made." Olson said.

"What's that?" Tori asked.

"Seeing my three kids together, like this, getting along." Olson answered, turning to Thuy. "I saw you, telling your story on T.V."

That's a shocker. Thuy thought. "You did?"

"We, all did." Jett said. "It was a wakeup call for all of us."

"How?" Thuy asked.

Olson held Thuy's hand, "I speak for all of us, by saying I'm sorry for the way we treated you all these years. I was young, stupid, and selfish. The way I acted towards your mother, I didn't lift a finger to get Mycha to back off. I'm sorry, baby girl."

Olson, turned to Jett and Tori, adding. "I'm sorry, you guys for allowing your mother to turn y'all against, Thuy. I should've set a better example, I didn't, and I'm so sorry."

Olson's words touched, Thuy. She grabbed some napkins off the table, drying her tears. She'd been waiting for this moment, all her life. "That's all I ever wanted. I'm willing to try if you guys are."

Everyone at the table held hands, Tori said. "Let's start over right now."

Everyone nodded in agreement, then their food arrived.

As they were eating their food Olson spoke. "Thuy, I reached out to your mother today, and apologized to her."

Thuy was blown away. Isla didn't mention to her, when they talked earlier. "How did that go?"

Olson, sighed before giving his answer. "She's not ready to forgive me, but she appreciated the gesture. She said, she'll work on it." His voice was mixed with disappointment and understanding. "She wished me happy birthday, so that's a start. There's something else you need to know."

"What's that?' Thuy asked.

"The reason I didn't come to the hospital, was because I was ashamed." Olson confessed.

"Of what?"

"Of what a horrible father I've been to you. That night at your house, when you asked me all those questions about you. I felt lower than shit. You're my daughter, I didn't know the basic facts about you. Not to mention, I was too much of a selfish coward, to comfort you after what that bastard Levi, did to you. I couldn't put you first, for one fucking minute. Please give me a chance." Olson pleaded.

"Will you give us a chance?" Tori said sincerely.

Thuy, pondered for a moment, "Okay cool, but after we finish eating this food."

Everyone laughed at Thuy's sense of humor, then said to Olson. "Happy Birthday!"

Jamila

Chapter 13

Sam was in Vida's room, sweating on top of her, using his dick to make her pussy creamy and sore, as she screamed his name. Their secret fuck session had been going on for three hours. Sam, then busted a huge nut deep inside Vida and collapsed on top of her.

"Oh shit." Sam panted, kissing his lady. "You are so fucking incredible!"

"Thanks baby." Vida said, snuggling in her man's arms. "Sam."

"Yes baby."

"You have made me the happiest woman in the world."

"I do my best." Sam grabbed her ass. "Vida, you do something to me. You drive me crazy. You make me take wild, crazy ass risks."

Vida giggled. "Great sex has that affect."

"I know right. You are sexy as fuck." Sam kissed Vida with more passion. "I just had to have you. Anytime, anywhere. On the desk, on the wall, on the couch or the kitchen counter. In the shower, on the floor, on the table. On top of the washer and dryer and on the stairway." He kissed her gently on the lips, as he listed all the places they fucked in the house.

"Oh my, the many places we've fucked while, Thuy, was gone." Vida's carefree mood changed when she glanced over at her phone and saw what time it was. "Oh shit."

"What's wrong, baby."

"It's one in the morning!"

"Oh shit!" Sam shrieked, as he and Vida, jumped out of bed rushing to get dressed. "Thuy might be on her way home from her dad's birthday dinner."

"I didn't hear her come in, we might be good." Vida hoped.

How could we hear, with all that screaming your ass was doing? Sam chuckled, quickly flashing back to how he had Vida screaming his name, with her legs and ass in the air.

"You got everything?" Vida asked.

Sam double checked to make sure he had everything. "Yeah, I

think so."

Vida gently cracked open the door and whispered, "Let's get you outta here before—"

"Before what?" Thuy caught them off guard, she was standing in the doorway, when Vida opened the door waiting for them to come out.

"Uh—Thuy, hey girl!" Vida stuttered nervously. "What are you doing here?"

"I own this house remember." Thuy answered, with a fake ass smile and turned to her big cousin. "Hi Sam. What are you doing here?"

Of course, Thuy already knew the answer. She just wanted to know how they were gonna talk their way out of this. Vida and Sam were terrible liars, especially Sam. *This shit is gonna be funny.* Thuy thought, grinning.

Sam started babbling senselessly and spat out the first lie he could think of. "Well—I was looking for you—and—"

"Oh nigga, don't even fucking try it." Thuy went ahead and put the no longer secret lovers out of their misery. "Both of y'all, nasty, sneaky asses are cold motherfucking busted. You negros didn't think I knew about y'all? Smelling your scents on each other all the damn time. Besides Vida, you've been drooling over Sam since the sixth grade. What the fuck y'all take me for? Some kind of idiot!"

"Why the fuck Bryn's ass gotta to be right all the motherfucking time?" Vida blurted out, annoyed that her secret crush was never really a secret.

"I feel you." Thuy agreed, because that shit did get annoying sometimes.

"I'm sorry we kept this from you, we didn't know how you, and the family would feel." Sam explained. "We were trying to figure out the right time to make our relationship public."

"Thuy, I don't want this to ruin our friendship, but Sam means everything to me." Vida pleaded. "I finally found a good man, who respects and appreciates me. I know this is a shock to you."

Sam pulled Vida into his arms. "That's right. I love this girl and I enjoy having her in my life."

Addicted to the Drama 2

Vida was taken aback when she heard Sam say the 'L' word in reference to her. "Sam, you love me?"

"Yes, baby girl, I love you."

Vida was so touched, she was about to cry. "Oh Sam, I love you, too."

The two pulled each other in a beautiful kiss. They were so deep into it, they completely forgot, Thuy, was still in their presence. "Uh—I'm still here."

Sam and Vida broke their kiss bashfully, Vida went back to pleading their case. "Look, Thuy, it couldn't be helped. Sam and I, love each other. Our relationship has so much passion. He makes me feel like a real woman. The way he looks at me. The way he holds me in his arms. The way he kisses me. Oh, the way he makes love to me, by pleasing my body, and by using his enormous dick giving it to me hard, slow, or—"

"Alright, that's enough. I don't wanna hear that nasty, ass shit." Thuy quickly shut it down. "Like, I wanna hear your ass talk about my cousin's dick?"

Sam was starting to get uncomfortable. "I think I should go."

"Oh, no Sam. Your black ass ain't going anywhere. You are spending the night." Thuy insisted.

"I am?" Sam was confused.

"Oh yes, because you two lovebirds, got a long day of cleaning ahead of y'all, at the crack of dawn." Sam and Vida, looked at Thuy like she was crazy. "Y'all motherfuckers heard me right. Since y'all nasty asses, think it's okay to fuck all over my house, y'all should have no problem cleaning this motherfucker from top to bottom!"

"What?" Vida looked, Thuy, up and down like she'd lost her damn mind.

"Bitch, you heard me. Y'all wanna be together. Y'all can start by cleaning every inch of my house together. Goodnight." Thuy, headed back to her bedroom.

"Goodnight." Sam and Vida said.

Sam shook his head, "I guess, I'll get my spare clothes from the guest room."

"Right after you take care of this." Vida said seductively and

Jamila

pulled Sam close to her. Sam pinned her against the wall and stuck his tongue in her mouth.

"Mmm." Sam moaned.

His dick got stiff and he was in the process of whipping it out, when Thuy, interrupted them.

"And no fucking in my hallway!" Thuy yelled, with authority, sticking her head out of her bedroom door. "Y'all wanna fuck, do it in a designated bedroom like normal motherfuckers. What a fucking shame I gotta make fucking rules in this motherfucking house."

When Sam and Vida, heard Thuy's bedroom door close, they busted out laughing.

"See Vida, I told you she'd take it well." Sam joked.

"Right." Vida replied, giggling.

She and Sam, went back in her room to abide by Thuy's rules.

Chapter 14

At the Restart Project Women's Center Library, a small meeting was being held, between the board members, Thuy, Vida and Ligia. Tylisha was also in attendance, because Ligia recommended her to decorate for the foundation's next event, which was a concert at the Lakewood Amphitheater.

"Have we come up with the acts for the concert?" Thuy asked Vida, who was looking through a list of entertainers.

"Not yet, still looking." Vida answered.

"Alrighty."

Ligia, was going over some notes, when she was surprised by a kiss from her hubby. "Hey baby. This is a surprise. What's up?"

"Just stopped by to see my favorite girl and drop off my donation." Vax, answered and waved an envelope in his hand.

"That's very nice of you. You're in luck. Ambrosia and Bryn, are coming this way." Tylisha said and pointed at their direction.

"Hello children." Ambrosia greeted.

"Hey, Ambrosia, hi Bryn." Everyone greeted, Bryn took his seat at the table.

"Vax buddy, how you doing?" Ambrosia hugged her longtime friend.

"Better than ever—Harley Mae." Vax teased, causing everyone to giggle.

Ambrosia, let her hood ghetto side take over. "Nigga, what did I tell you about screaming my government out like that?"

"Girl, quit with the bougie shit." Vax shot back, handing Ambrosia the envelope with his ten-million- dollar donation check inside.

"Uh huh." Ambrosia, opened the envelope and took a peek at the check. "You lucky we go way back and you're a huge ass donor." She turned to everyone at the table and asked. "What's going on?"

"Going through the celebrity list looking for performers." Vida informed.

"Time to take my leave." Vax said, giving Ligia a goodbye kiss.

Jamila

"See you at home."

"Bye baby." Ligia said.

"I'll be in the office if y'all need me." Ambrosia said, walking away.

"Alright, Harley Mae." Everyone at the table teased.

Ambrosia turned around, responding with playful authority. "Don't let Vax get y'all fucked up in here."

"What do we got so far?" Bryn asked.

"Marsha, is going to speak at our luncheon next week and at the concert." Thuy said.

She and Vida were so thankful, for the opportunity to work with the retired detective that helped them during their traumatic ordeals.

"Hey Ligia. Why don't you sing at the concert?" Thuy suggested.

"That's a great idea." Tylisha agreed. "What a better way to get your message across than to have a board member perform."

Ligia hadn't sung in public in a good little while. The last time was when she sung her vows to Vax, at their wedding. Along with her graceful singing voice Ligia's erotic beauty, long curly light brown hair, with a subtle touch of red, and gray eyes were the reasons for her successful beauty pageant runs.

Ligia loved singing, so she decided to go for it. "What the hell, it's for a good cause."

"This is a wonderful thing you guys are doing. Putting together this concert to honor survivors of sexual assault and domestic violence, and raising money for the charities to help with these issues." Tylisha complimented.

"And thank you Tylisha, for decorating for the event. I know it's a big job." Bryn said.

"It was my pleasure. It's for a great cause. That reminds me, is there gonna be a segment where the survivors tell their stories?" Tylisha wondered.

"Why in the hell didn't we think of that?" Ligia kicked herself for not coming up with that obvious idea.

"Y'all should do a segment after every performance. Give these issues a face, a voice. Show the real people. Give them a chance to tell their stories." Tylisha explained.

"I feel what you're saying." Thuy agreed.

"Look here." Vida pointed at a name on the list. "Hope the singer, we can have her perform. She's also a rape and domestic abuse survivor."

"Her story was powerful." Ligia remembered. "Do you think she'll get on board?"

"Only one way to find out." Bryn pulled out his phone and stepped away to make the call.

"Thuy, I saw your interview on the Orlando Wall Show and another one you did with Macy Bowe." Tylisha said. "On Macy's show, you talked about that dude who tried to rape you. What was his name? I forgot, but I think it started with an L."

"Levi Parsans." Thuy answered.

"I remember that name." Ligia said. "When I started out as a substitute teacher, one of my former student's ex-stepfather's sister-in-law was related to him. She knew he was capable of rape. It was no secret in his family, but they all looked the other way. Sadly, it's very common."

"He actually raped me." Vida added.

"What? No way!" Tylisha was blown away.

"He raped me, while he and Thuy, were still together." Vida said.

"Levi, was the guy that raped you?" Ligia asked Vida. "I thought it was your ex-boyfriend, Thuy, and Bryn rescued you from."

"He did too." Vida confirmed. "You see in addition to beating my ass, he thought just because I was his girlfriend, living in his house, he could take sex anytime he wanted. Not giving a fuck if I wanted it or not."

"I'm sorry you had to go through that." Tylisha said with compassion. "I'm glad you made it out of that situation in one piece."

"Barely." Vida sighed at the memories of her humiliating abuse. "The last time I saw him he beat my ass, because I told him I was leaving, when I found out he got another woman pregnant. After he beat and raped me, he left me in the middle of that living room floor

Jamila

to die. Then he walked out of the house like hurting me wasn't shit to him. It wasn't easy, but I managed to find my phone. I called, Thuy, and told her what happened. She and Bryn, drove in the middle of the night from here to Charlotte, to take me away from that bastard, I never looked back." Bryn came back and took his seat.

He and Thuy, rubbed Vida's back in a loving manner.

"You three guys are loyal to the end, I see that." Tylisha admired.

"That's right." Thuy said. "If it wasn't for these two, I wouldn't be sitting here right now." After referring to the night of the shooting, Thuy, pointed at Bryn. "If it wasn't for this dude, Levi, would've raped me. I was scared to report it, because I was afraid no one would believe me. I knew no one at our first high school wouldn't have."

After they testified at the trial, Thuy, Bryn and Vida, had to transfer to another school and things were great.

"Why not?" Tylisha asked.

Thuy sighed. "I was unfairly labeled a hoe, because of my bastard ex and first time Connor Hale."

"Let me guess. He told you he loved you and he'd never tell a soul what y'all did, but it ended up all over school, after he not so coincidently distanced himself from you, and eventually dumped you?" Tylisha recited one of the many trials and tribulations of teenage girls. The reasons they grew up to become broken and damaged women with trust issues.

"Exactly and Levi, was one of his friends he told what a great fuck I was."

"That motherfucker!" Ligia hissed.

"Whatever happened to Levi?" Tylisha asked.

"He ended up with a long prison sentence." Thuy answered. "Four girls came forward besides Vida and myself. The weird thing is, that he committed suicide two weeks before his release."

"Two weeks before his release? Something's funny about that." Tylisha said with suspicion. She pointed at Thuy and Vida, then made another suggestion. "Why don't you two share your stories at the concert, too?"

72

Thuy looked over at Vida, "What do you say?"

"It can't hurt us anymore." Vida replied. "We might as well tell it, we've been through worse."

Jamila

Addicted to the Drama 2

Chapter 15

It was that time of the year again, May 2nd, Macal spent the night at Tylisha's house, and was now getting ready to visit his mother's grave. This year, the day was very awkward, because it was also his girlfriend's birthday.

Macal, didn't know what he was gonna do. He ordered a bouquet of red roses for Thuy. He still, didn't know how he was gonna get through the day. Or how he'd deal with having a girlfriend, whose birthday is on the same day, as the anniversary of his mother's death. His phone rang, interrupting his thoughts.

"Hello." Thuy greeted.

"Happy birthday, baby girl." Macal greeted with a smile.

"I called to check on you and thank you for the roses." Thuy understood Macal, might not be in a festive mood for her birthday.

She appreciated the roses and wanted to see how he was doing before visiting his mother's grave.

"You deserve it." Macal insisted. "I'm at Tylisha's house getting ready."

"That's right, you told me, you were spending the night there." Thuy reminded herself. "Call if you need anything okay."

"Okay, enjoy your day, baby girl."

"Thanks."

After the call ended Macal, heard a knock at the door. "Come in."

Tylisha walked in and asked. "Ready to go? Grandma Doris called, she's ready for us to pick her up."

"Yeah, I was talking to Thuy. Wishing her a happy birthday." Macal said.

"I just sent her a birthday text."

"I feel so bad." Macal shook his head. "Thuy, is an amazing girl and I can't do anything special for her."

Tylisha, sat on the bed next to Macal, and said with understanding. "I know today is conflicting, Momma's death falling on, Thuy's birthday."

"Thuy, is so understanding of my feelings today. Truthfully, that's what makes me feel worse."

"You do know, we're not gonna be at the gravesite all day." Tylisha hinted.

Macal, got the message. "I get what you're saying. Thuy's special, it's hard to explain. When I'm with her, I feel like a whole different person. I love spending time with her. I know this might be TMI, but we sleep in the same bed and nothing happens. We just sleep in each other's arms. We haven't even had sex yet, and I'm cool with that."

"Awe my big brother is trying to grow up." Tylisha said in a cute baby voice.

"What do you mean?" Macal asked.

"What you just described, is what we grownups call intimacy."

"Intimacy?" Macal, sounded like it was a foreign word. "How is that intimacy and we didn't fuck?"

His ass is beyond clueless! Tylisha began to break down the concept of intimacy. "What we grownups mean by intimacy, is that it's not just sex. Sure that's another form of intimacy. Intimacy also means feeling safe and secure, revealing yourself emotionally and mentally with someone. Building a deep connection with that person. Shit like that."

"Right, right."

Tylisha, went on with her in depth explanation about intimacy versus fucking. "Example, yes I know you're still fucking Lolette. You need to stop that nasty ass shit, but I digress. When we were in New Orleans, you tossed that hoe on her ass. Why? Because with Lolette it's just fucking, no connection at all. With Thuy, even though y'all have never fucked, y'all share a connection. You'd rather have, Thuy, in your arms watching movies and T.V., than be on top of that bitch blowing her back out. That should tell you something." Tylisha heard her phone ring and dug into her purse. She saw who the caller was, rolled her eyes, and stuffed it back in her purse. "This nigga."

"Who was that?"

"Milton."

"What the fuck does he want?"

"To see the kids."

"I guess Enzo didn't beat his ass good enough."

Tylisha laughed at Macal's sarcastic comment, before he asked the serious question.

"All kidding aside, what do you think, about him wanting to see the kids?"

"I don't know." Tylisha sighed. "He's their father, so he does have that right. I just don't want my babies getting hurt."

"Those kids come first, fuck what he wants." Macal snapped.

In Macal's mind, Milton, didn't deserve the honor or privilege to be a father. However, he did understand why Tylisha would be torn.

"But if you are considering it, talk to Milton first to fill him out. Then talk to the kids. When both sides are ready, have them meet at a mutual place, so there won't be any problems."

"That's actually a good idea." Tylisha agreed. "The crazy part is, it came from your fucked up ass."

"Awe thanks, Tylisha, for thinking so highly of me." Macal, relied with sarcasm.

"Yeah, you a fucked-up nigga, but I'm glad you're my brother." Tylisha hugged Macal. "I can't imagine having a better one. I love you." She kissed him on the cheek.

"I love you too, baby girl." Macal said and the Kilborn, siblings went on their way to visit their mother.

Jamila

Chapter 16

"Thanks for the birthday dinner, momma." Thuy said.

She decided to keep her birthday simple this year. Isla cooked all her favorites for her birthday dinner. Greg made her an ice cream birthday cake. At the dinner was Sam, Vida, and Bryn. Earlier today Olson, Jett, and Tori took Thuy, to a matinée to see Black Panther.

"Anything for my birthday baby." Isla said, as she gathered all the plates and put them in the sink.

"Yeah, Mrs. Dawson. You put your foot in it." Bryn complimented.

"Thanks Bryn." Isla said.

The food was so good, Sam, wanted seconds. "Aunt Isla, is there anymore macaroni and cheese, collard greens, friend chicken—"

"Boy here." Isla already had Sam's to go plate, all wrapped up, and handed it to him. "You just as bad as your daddy with that stomach."

"Ain't it the truth?" Vida agreed, pointing at Sam. "Cooking for this guy, is like being a chef at Golden Corral." She turned to Sam, "I'm teaching you how to cook tomorrow."

"Yes baby." Sam kissed Vida.

"Great ice cream cake, Greg. It was delicious." Thuy said.

"Anything for the birthday girl." Greg said.

Then the doorbell rang. "Thuy will you be so kind and get the door." Isla said.

"Sure." Thuy, got out of her seat to answer the door and was met with an unexpected surprise. "What in the world?"

Macal, gave Thuy a bouquet of red roses and a teddy bear. Behind him was Ligia, singing Happy Birthday along with Vax accompanying on his saxophone. When he came back from visiting Belinda's grave Macal, called Ligia and Vax, to help him put together the last-minute surprise.

Thuy was touched, Ligia's voice was sweet and beautiful. Vax's saxophone playing was spectacular. When the song ended, Thuy, rushed straight to the musically gifted couple and hugged them. "That was so amazing! Thanks, Ligia and Vax, y'all were great. So much talent!"

"Hey, wait a minute. What about your man?" Macal teased.

"Oh, my bad." Thuy, teased back, then hugged Macal and kissed him. "Thanks baby." She looked over at her people, who were all smiles and concluded. "Y'all knew about this didn't you?"

"Yeah!" They confessed.

Thuy, turned back to Macal. "No wonder you knew to come here and Bryn insisted on being the one to drive us here." Thuy gave Macal another kiss. "Thanks for the surprise. How did it go today at your mother's—"

"Shh!" He interrupted. He knew Thuy, was concerned, but he didn't want her worrying about him. "Today is all about you. Come, I have a surprise for you."

"A surprise? Great, what is it?" Thuy jumped up and down, cheering with excitement.

"Now baby girl if I told you it wouldn't be a surprise." Macal smiled.

"Right." Thuy turned to her people, "Well I'm about to take off to parts unknown. Vida pack my cake, leftovers, presents and bring them home."

"Okay, Thuy." Vida said. "Enjoy the rest of your birthday."

"I will." Thuy smiled.

She and Macal, went on their way, arm and arm in romantic bliss.

****

Macal and Thuy, arrived at their destination. Thuy, was truly surprised. "A helicopter ride? Are you fucking kidding me?"

"Come on Thuy, it'll be fun." Macal took Thuy, by the hand, and led towards the pilot. "You flew on airplanes hundreds of times."

"That's different."

"Oh really, how?"

"Well—uh—"

"Well—uh—" Macal, slapped Thuy, on the ass. "Get that fine sexy ass inside."

Thuy, cut her eyes at Macal. "Look at you giving me orders on my birthday."

"Whatever you love it."

"Good evening." The pilot greeted. "My name is Robert, I'll be your pilot." He turned to Thuy, "I understand, that you're the birthday girl?"

"Yes, I am." Thuy answered smiling.

Robert turned to Macal, "You're right sir. This beautiful, stunning, young lady deserves this special treat."

"Somebody's getting lucky tonight." Thuy whispered to Macal.

Macal's dick jumped, at the thought of finally getting a taste of Thuy's pussy. "Really?"

"Really." Thuy confirmed giving Macal's dick a quick inconspicuous squeeze, before they boarded the helicopter.

Robert helped them get settled in the back. He made sure they had an excellent view and the champagne was prepared as requested. "You guys just let me do the flying. All y'all gotta do is relax and enjoy the view."

"Thanks." Macal and Thuy, said simultaneously.

The helicopter took off, Thuy took a big gulp of her champagne, like a shot in order to calm her nerves. She fixed herself another glass to really enjoy the taste, then made herself comfortable in Macal's arms. "What a beautiful view." She said in awe.

"Isn't it?" Macal agreed.

During the helicopter ride the sounds of *Come and Talk to me* and *Forever My Lady* by *Jodeci* were heard.

When *What About Us* came on she asked Macal. "You actually had the pilot play songs from my favorite R&B male group?" Without waiting for an answer, she wrapped her arms around him, and kissed him. "You really know how to treat a woman."

"I do my best." Macal replied modestly. "Look outside at the sky." He instructed.

Thuy, did as she was told and looked outside at the sky. She saw the colorful fireworks light up with words that spelled out:

Jamila

Happy Birthday, Thuy! I love you, baby girl! Reading those words made her feel like a queen. She had to be sure of what she was reading and asked her king. "Really, do you love me?"

Macal caressed Thuy's hand, "Yes, baby girl, I love you. You are my everything. I love having you in my life. I want you to remain in my life. Thuy Ellis, I love you, baby girl. Happy birthday!"

"Oh Macal Kilborn, I love you too." Thuy said.

Macal pulled her into a deep passionate kiss. This was the best birthday in Thuy's life. This man put his awkwardness aside, just to go all out for her. No man had ever gone out of his way for her. She couldn't help but love this man back.

It's official, I'm definitely giving him some pussy tonight!

Chapter 17

"Whoo, hoo!" Thuy, squealed with joy, as she and Macal, entered his bedroom at his penthouse. "Thanks for taking me."

"I knew you'd like it." Macal kissed Thuy. "Happy birthday, my queen."

"Thanks, my king." Thuy said.

Macal pulled her close and stuck his tongue in her mouth. During the kiss she felt something in Macal's lower region getting hard and stiff.

She knew what that meant. "I think somebody else wanna wish me a very happy birthday."

"He does." Macal answered for his friend between his legs.

"Alright." Thuy said, getting down on her knees.

She unzipped Macal's pants, letting them fall to the floor. She pulled down his boxers and there was the most beautiful dick, she'd ever seen in her life. It was nine inches, thick, and curved.

Damn, I hit the jackpot. Thuy thought.

She stuck her tongue out and licked all over his dick. Thuy, didn't think she could get the whole thing in her mouth, so she took in a little at a time, until she got comfortable enough to move further down the shaft. She used her right hand to juggle his balls.

Thuy bobbled her head up and down, on the dick nice and slow, using her saliva to get it nice and wet. She loved sucking dick. It was her favorite sex act to perform and sucking Macal's dick made it even more fun because of the challenge. Thuy felt Macal's cum explode in her mouth, she swallowed it in one big gulp.

"Shit girl!" Macal panted, helping Thuy, off the floor. "That was some fiyah head."

"Thanks." Thuy said.

She got undressed and Macal followed suit. Now completely nude Macal, couldn't take his eyes off Thuy's body. Her fat ass, those big juicy, succulent titties, and thick thighs.

"You are so fucking sexy girl." Macal complimented.

"Damn!" Was all Thuy could say, when she saw how well built Macal's body was. "I need you on top of me now!"

Jamila

"Alright, baby!" Macal said.

The couple climbed into bed. Macal climbed on top of Thuy. He used his dick to enter Thuy's pussy and gave it some rough strokes.

Thuy's body began to shake, she screamed in ecstasy. This dick wasn't anything she had ever felt before. Macal fucked her like he knew where all her spots were. She opened her legs wider, grabbed a hold of his ass and pulled him deeper inside her.

Macal grabbed Thuy's right titty and put it in his mouth. He sucked on the nipple, as he kept his pace. He used his dick to explore every inch of the pussy, his pussy. He did a deep circular motion while still deep inside her. He smashed both titties together and licked both the nipples.

"Oooh—ah—" Thuy came.

Thuy's pussy was super tight. Macal thought his dick was about to explode. He didn't wanna get out of this breathtaking pussy, but he couldn't hold out any longer. He busted a fat nut, filling her pussy up. There was so much cum it flowed freely out of Thuy's pussy.

"Wow!" Thuy panted, as Macal rolled off top of her.

Macal pulled Thuy into his arms and planted a post sex kiss on her. "Your pussy must be made out of platinum girl."

Thuy giggled. "I'm sorry baby."

"For what?"

"Making you wait this long."

"It's all good baby."

"I missed out on a lot." Thuy could honestly say that was the best sex of her life. Macal was not going anywhere. His dick was out of this world. "Macal?"

"Yes baby?"

"I want some more."

Music to my ears. "Good because I need some more of this bomb ass pussy." Macal gave Thuy's clit a quick rub. "After we watch this movie I picked up." He climbed out of bed to set up the movie.

"What movie?" Thuy's question was answered when Macal finished the setup and she saw the T.V. screen. "You bought *Mommie*

84

Dearest?"

"I had to get it." Macal said, rejoining Thuy in bed. "That movie grew on me."

"Told you." Thuy snuggled in Macal's arms. "Good thinking. We need a break before we start fucking again."

"Watching our movie."

Thuy nodded and replied. "Yeah, our movie."

Jamila

Chapter 18

Shit, I'm sore. Thuy woke up in aching pain, but in a good way. It seemed she and Macal, had spent the whole night making up for all the times not having sex. That man was the best lover she'd ever had. The dick, the stamina, and his head game. She didn't know her body could bend in all the positions he put her in. Some of them she had no clue even existed. With a smile on her face, Thuy, rolled over to greet her man.

"Good morning, Macal." To her surprise he wasn't in bed. "Macal—Macal!" Thuy called loudly.

"I'm in the office, baby!" Macal yelled his answer.

"Okay." She yelled back.

Thuy climbed out of bed and looked through Macal's dresser drawer, in search of something to cover her naked body. She found an oversized black t-shirt and put it on. She walked out of the bedroom, to find Macal. She searched all over the penthouse and found him in his office upstairs.

Macal, was sitting at his desk, wearing gray sweatpants, and no shirt hard at work. Thuy, walked over to him and gave him a kiss. "Good morning."

"Good morning, baby." He greeted, smiling. He stuck his hand under Thuy's t-shirt and rubbed her ass. *No panties—great.* He thought.

"Sausage, egg and cheese sandwich?" Thuy saw Macal's plate.

"Your plate is in the microwave." Macal pointed at the corner.

Thuy went over to the microwave, to get her plate, and fixed herself a cup of coffee. She took her seat on the couch, taking a sip of her coffee. "This coffee was needed. Forever the working man I see."

"The hustle never stops." Macal said, finishing his sandwich.

"You can say that again." Thuy finished her sandwich and sipped on her coffee, as she looked through her phone at her news feed. She found something interesting. "What do we have here?" She commented under her breath.

"Did you say something, baby?" Macal looked up because he

thought he'd heard Thuy speak.

"Oh, I'm strolling through my news feed." Thuy said. "I see that Jeromy's property is gonna be auctioned off."

"Good for his ass."

Thuy continued to stroll through the news feed, when her petty senses started to tingle. "Hey, Macal. How long have you been living in this penthouse?"

"This is one of my rental properties, I moved in here about six months after the car accident." Macal answered. "In fact, it was the same day I bought that car from you."

"Don't you wanna live in a house again?"

"Gee I never thought about it. It would be nice. Problem is where would I have the time to go house hunting?" Macal asked.

"You don't really have to go out and house hunt if you don't mind me making a suggestion."

"I'm listening."

Thuy strutted towards Macal and sat on his lap. "One of Jeromy's properties that's being auctioned off is his mansion. If you end up being the highest bidder, the house is yours."

She must be joking. Macal gave Thuy a crazy look. "Baby do you think that's a good idea? Me, your new man, buying your ex-fiancé's house, especially with the kind of history y'all have?"

"I don't see the problem." Thuy shrugged.

"What about the memories that house will bring you?" Macal gave Thuy's ass a hard rub. "For obvious reasons, if I buy this house I want you in it with me."

"Not if you tear it down and build a new on the exact same spot." Thuy added to her original suggestion.

Shit, she even makes being petty sexy. Macal caught onto Thuy's plan. "Oh, I see. You wanna pull the former Mrs. Tiger Woods with a twist, huh?"

"Yeah." Thuy confessed unapologetically.

"So, I buy the house. Tear it down and build the house I want."

"Right."

"Then Tylisha can decorate it." Macal then decided to get in on the petty act. "I can also bid on some properties, fix them up a bit, and make an attractive offer for future investors."

"Exactly, good plan."

Thuy got off Macal's lap and took her seat back on the couch to check her news feed again. She saw something that changed her mood.

Macal noticed instantly. "What's wrong, baby?"

"It's a story about a former client of mine I had to drop—Jake Simon."

"Jake Simon? He was a number one draft pick, a few years back, he ended up being a huge bust." Macal recalled.

"A huge bust is being nice about it." Thuy slightly exaggerated. "That boy was a hot ass mess. He was selfish, all he did was party and make babies. Please don't get me started on his performance on the field."

"Oh, I remember." Macal nodded. "That nigga cost me over ten thousand dollars. What's going on with him now?"

"He's broke." Thuy said with pity. "This happens too often. These kids playing pro ball. Getting all this money and don't know what to do with it. Mix that with no guidance and discipline, that shit ends up a complete fucking disaster. Or they spend it up like it's going out of style."

"Or trust the wrong person with their finances and business affairs." Macal added.

"It's so sad, I see it happen all the time." Thuy sighed. "If only there was a way to prevent this type of shit from happening."

Maybe there is. Macal made a mental note.

"I'll let you get back to work."

"Hey—hey—hey." Macal caught up with Thuy, before she walked out the door, and pulled her in his arms. "Where do you think you're going?"

"Back to bed." Thuy answered. "Unless you wanna join me and make love to me again."

"Hell yeah, I wanna make love to you again, but why go all the way back to the bedroom." Macal pushed Thuy back one the couch and pounced on top of her like she was prey. "I can fuck the shit out of right here, right now."

Jamila

"Oh yeah." Thuy spread her legs as far apart as she could and let Macal have his way with her.

Chapter 19

"So, what's the word, Dr. Moon?" Ligia asked nervously with Tylisha by her side.

"Well Ligia it looks like we have to run more tests." Dr. Moon said.

"Why, what's the problem?" Tylisha asked.

"It seems like the cancer cells are stabilized." Dr Moon answered.

"What does that mean?" Ligia asked.

"There's no improvement, but the cancer hasn't been spreading. That's why I want to perform more tests to see exactly what we're dealing with." Dr. Moon explained. "I also want to change your prescription."

"Alright." Ligia said.

Dr. Moon wrote out Ligia's prescription and handed it to her. "Here you go, your appointment is scheduled for next Friday at 11:30 a.m."

"Thanks, have a nice day." Ligia said.

"You too." Dr. Moon said.

After Ligia's doctor's appointment, Tylisha, drove her to fill her prescription. Afterwards they went to Buffalo Wild Wings to get something to eat.

Tylisha was pigging out, but Ligia barely touched her food. Her mind was on everything but eating.

"Are you, okay?" Tylisha asked.

"I'm okay." Ligia answered unconvincingly. "I just have a lot on my mind." She sighed and shook her head. "Shit, I don't know what the fuck is gonna happen."

"Your results are stable."

"But, for how long? Am I gonna beat this shit, or is it gonna get worse and take me the fuck out?"

"We're not gonna think about that right now, okay." Tylisha said. "We're gonna take this one day at a time."

Ligia nodded. "I love my life, Tylisha. My family, my friends, my career. I don't wanna lose it." Tears started to flow from her eyes, Ligia confessed her true feelings. "Tylisha, I've never been so scared and terrified in all my life."

Tylisha squeezed Ligia's hand, "It's gonna be alright. Listen to me, you got cancer. That bitch don't got you, remember that."

"Right." Ligia grabbed a napkin, wiped her tears, and started eating her food. "Enough about me, let's talk about you. What's up?"

Tylisha shook her head. "You don't need to hear my problems."

"Come on, you can tell me." Ligia insisted. "You've been by my side during this cancer fight. Let me be a friend to you. What's going on, are you and Enzo having problems?"

"No, things are great between us."

"Is it Macal, Mrs. Blair, or the kids?"

"Grandma Doris is fine. Other than Macal, still being his hoe self, he and Thuy are good. As far as the kids, I don't even know where to start." Tylisha took a few sips of her Pepsi.

"What's wrong?"

"You got enough on your plate." Tylisha shook her head.

"Tylisha, just because I'm sick, doesn't mean I can't be a good supportive friend to you. What's going on with the kids?" Ligia asked.

"Alright, I'll tell you. I'm surprised Enzo didn't tell you."

"Tell me what?"

"Milton's back." Tylisha said.

Ligia's eyes stretched, "Your ex-husband?"

"Yeah, that nigga." Tylisha rolled her eyes.

"When did he come back?"

"Literally, right before our trip to New Orleans." Tylisha answered. "Ever since then he's been riding me about seeing the kids."

"What did you tell him?"

"I told his ass hell to the motherfucking no! I don't want his deadbeat, junkie, fucked up ass around my babies."

"He's on drugs?" This shit was getting insane to Ligia. "And my cancer-stricken ass, thought I had it rough." She shook her head with pity. "Do you think it's true?"

"According to Thuy's sources Milton got kicked off his last few

92

teams, cause of drugs, and his now ex-wife halfway cleaned him out in the divorce." Tylisha ate one of her wings.

"Honey, I understand your concerns. Assuming the drug shit is true." Ligia said.

"Exactly."

"I'm guessing Enzo knows about this."

Tylisha let out a laugh. "Know about it, he beat Milton's ass!"

"I gotta hear this." Ligia said.

She knew Enzo could fight. Tylisha filled her in on everything that went down at her house when Macal and Thuy, took the kids out for the day.

"So, what you gonna do?"

"I don't know." Tylisha was extremely conflicted. "Welton and Ayla, are his kids too, but I don't wanna gamble."

Tylisha's dilemma made Ligia think about her own father. "I understand you wanna protect your children but let me share something with you. My daddy died in prison, when I was five months pregnant with Amery."

"How tragic, I'm sorry to hear that." Tylisha sympathized.

"Oh, don't feel bad." Ligia replied nonchalantly. "It wasn't like he was in my life much growing up."

"Explain."

"When momma was pregnant with me daddy pulled a Tiki Barber."

"Your daddy left your momma for a young hot blonde, while you were still in the womb." Tylisha guessed.

"Right." Ligia confirmed. "Sasha and daddy were very close. She was devastated when he left. Me on the other hand. Like the saying goes, you can't miss what you never had. Daddy was so wrapped up with her, he basically forgot all about us."

"Trust me, I know and lived it." Tylisha could definitely relate. That's why she's dealing with this Milton bullshit now. "How did he end up in prison?"

"He walked in on her fucking another dude and he killed him. His ass spent all that time in prison, begging that white hoe to stay with him." Ligia rolled her eyes with disgust.

"How old were you when he went to prison?"

Ligia had to do some quick mental math. "Let's see, the last time I saw him before he went to prison I was five. Three years after that he went to prison, so age eight. He sent that bitch letters all the fucking time. From ages eight to twenty-one I only got seven."

"Thirteen years and the nigga only sent you seven letters?" Tylisha thought that was fucked up. No wonder Ligia thought so highly of Nico. He was really the only father she'd ever known. "Did you visit him?"

"Twice." Ligia held up two fingers. "Once when I was in the eighth grade and when he was about to die. I took that chance to tell him everything about himself. How he made me feel. What he missed out on, everything." Ligia took a minute to catch her breath before making her point. "What I'm trying to say is maybe you should give Welton and Ayla, a chance to express themselves to Milton. Ask them how they feel about him. They might have questions they wanna ask him. Let them have that opportunity."

Tylisha had to admit, Ligia made sense. Welton and Ayla, deserved answers to whatever questions they had. "I'll talk to Milton and see how it goes before I talk to the kids."

"Good thinking." Ligia agreed.

Tylisha, got out of her seat for a quick second, to give Ligia a hug. "Thanks girl."

"That's what friends are for, thanks for standing by my side."

Chapter 20

"We really balled out, didn't we?" Macal cheered as he carried, Thuy, on piggyback in his penthouse office. They'd just returned from the auction of Jeromy's properties.

"Yes, we did." Thuy cheered. "Congrats on getting the house, baby."

"No, thank you for the tip, baby." Macal put Thuy down and kissed her. "The house is all set to be torn down next week."

"Let's not forget the two rental properties." Thuy added.

"And that lime green Ferrari you're gonna donate to charity." Macal mentioned. "Who knew being petty could be so much fun and profitable."

"Told you." Thuy looked around and saw the chess game under a table. "You play chess?"

"Yes, I do. You?" Macal asked.

"Oh yes."

"Let's makes this chess game really interesting." Macal pulled the game out from under the table.

"How interesting?" Thuy took a seat at the table.

"Let's play strip chess." Macal suggested, setting up the game.

"I like the sound of that." Thuy giggled. "How does this work?"

"Let's say when I jump your piece, you strip and when you jump my piece, I'll do the same. Of course, checkmate still applies, but you also win if your opponent ends up wearing nothing." Macal set the rules.

"I'm down and to be fair." Thuy took off her golden custom made Italian pumps.

"Alright." Macal agreed, taking off his black designer shoes and socks.

"Who goes first?" Thuy asked.

Macal took his seat, "Beautiful queens first."

Thuy giggled. "Okay."

Thuy, made her first move by moving her pawn forward. Then Macal followed suit. He was confident that he was gonna win and see, Thuy's naked banging body. He had inherited his skills from his mother's side.

As the game went on Macal, realized this game was tougher than he thought. He ended up in nothing but his boxers. Thuy was in her purple bra and matching G-string. Macal recalled a Facebook meme he saw a while back.

It read: *The government is playing you, like a naked woman playing chess. The distraction is there, but the game is real.*

"This shit is getting real." Macal said.

"You don't say." Thuy pulled out her left titty and gave her nipple a quick lick, winked at Macal, and put her titty back.

She's trying to fuck with me. Macal made his move to stay in the game. "There."

Thuy gave Macal a look, jumped Macal's bishop, and yelled. "Checkmate."

Macal's mouth hung wide open. He was completely dumbfounded. "Damn girl, you got my ass." He stood up to drop his drawers letting his dick and balls hang.

"Well I did win fifteen out of twenty chess tournaments in my lifetime." Thuy bragged.

Macal pulled Thuy up, sat back in his chair, and slung her over his lap, giving her ass a hard smack. "Naughty girl, you hustled me."

"Ouch!" Thuy screamed in pain, getting out of Macal's lap. "Oh, and not telling me your momma was a chess grandmaster, wasn't a trick to get me out of my thong?" She rubbed her ass, where Macal, left his handprint.

"Tylisha told you?" Macal asked.

"Grandma Doris." Thuy corrected. "I guess we kind of hustled each other." She laughed.

Macal, joined in on the laughter. "Right."

"What do you think we two hustlers need to do now?"

"I think you need to get out of that thong and bra and let me tear that ass up." Macal said with authority, stroking his dick.

"Yes baby." Thuy smiled, taking off her bra and thong.

Macal bent Thuy over on the couch and forced his dick deep inside her. Thuy held onto the couch and let Macal blow her back out.

Addicted to the Drama 2

"Ah." Thuy moaned as she came.

"That's right baby. Cum on this dick."

"Ah, oh yes."

Macal's phone started to ring and that pissed them off. "Shit," Macal rolled his eyes.

His intent was to ignore the ringing and keep fucking, but suddenly he felt the urge to be petty. He took his dick out of Thuy's sweet pussy and gave her a kiss. "Watch this baby."

Macal found his pants and dug into his pocket for his phone. He saw who it was and answered. "Me and my woman are fucking. Call back some other time." He hung up the phone without a guilt and turned it off.

Thuy let out a loud, maniacal, sexy cackle. "That was telling them. You've been hanging out with me too long. You are starting to be pettier than me."

"Uh huh." Macal forced his tongue in Thuy's mouth and gave her ass another slap. "Now get that ass upstairs and in my fucking bed."

"Yes baby." Thuy obeyed Macal's orders and dashed out of the office, up the stairs, in to the bedroom, with Macal behind her enjoying the view of her bouncing ass cheeks.

The two jumped in bed devouring each other, unaware that Lolette, was on the other side of the penthouse door, clearly hearing the loud fucking noises from the blissful couple. She couldn't believe what this nigga had the balls to say to her on the phone.

"No, his bitch ass didn't." Lolette was fuming. "That's it, no more fucking around. It's about to be on and motherfucking popping." She stormed off already plotting how she was gonna take down, Thuy Fucking Ellis!

Jamila

Chapter 21

"Thanks, baby for coming." Tylisha kissed Enzo, letting him in the house.

Today was the day she was gonna talk to the kids about Milton. For the past few weeks she and Milton had been talking, trying to put the past behind them. She convinced him that it was best if she talked to the kids first. When they were ready she'd set up a meeting.

"Anything for you, baby." Enzo said. "Are you sure you wanna do this?"

"I think I'm ready." Tylisha convinced herself. "Ligia really opened my eyes."

"She told me she told you about her father." Enzo took a seat on the couch.

Tylisha made herself comfortable in Enzo's arms. "She helped me understand the importance of closure."

"That visit was intense as fuck." Enzo shook his head.

"You were there?"

"Of course. We were newlyweds, Ligia was pregnant." Enzo said. "I had to calm her down. That stress was not good for her and Amery."

"Ligia's right." Tylisha said. "The kids need to face Milton and let him know how they feel."

Enzo made a mental note to thank Ligia for being a great friend to Tylisha. It was nice to see the maturity between the love of his life and his ex-wife who he shared a special friendship and son with. These two important ladies in his life were not only getting along, but also building a strong friendship, and supporting each other.

"Are you ready?" Enzo asked.

Tylisha let out a huge sigh preparing herself for anything. "I'm as ready as I'm gonna be."

"Remember, I'm right here." Enzo rubbed Tylisha's back.

"Okay." Tylisha stood up and called out for her children. "Kids come down here!"

"Yes momma!" Welton and Ayla responded and made their

way downstairs.

"Have a seat." Tylisha instructed. "There's something I need to talk to you two about."

"What you wanna talk about momma?" Ayla asked.

This is it, now or never. "It's about your father." She managed to say.

"What about him?" Ayla asked with curiosity.

"What does he want?" Welton snapped with anger.

"He wants to see you guys." Tylisha answered. "He wants to get to know you and..."

"I don't wanna see him." Welton interrupted.

Even though he was about five years old when Milton left, he clearly remembered the pain, and suffering he put his mother and their family through. He hated Milton for it and had no interest in seeing him at all. As far as Welton was concerned they were just fine without him.

"Welton just calm down." Enzo said.

"No, he thinks he can just come up in here like everything is all good. He can forget it. He can stay where he at! We don't need him!" Welton hopped off the couch and went straight to his room in a huff.

"Welton!" Tylisha cried out.

"I'll see if he's okay." Ayla offered.

Tylisha hugged her mini-me and admired her compassion and loyalty to her loved ones. "Thanks baby girl."

When Ayla left Tylisha plumped on the couch. "And here I am thinking it was gonna be a disaster." She commented with sarcasm.

"What now?" Enzo asked and let Tylisha get comfortable in his arms.

Tylisha gave her analysis on the situation. "Ayla seems to be going with the flow. That's to be expected since she was only two when Milton left. Welton, I don't know—" During her long pause an idea popped into her head. It was a long shot, but it was worth a try. "Unless—"

"Unless what?"

Tylisha pulled out her phone to make a call. "I think I might

know someone who'll be able to soften Welton up a bit."
"Who?"

****

Tylisha laid in Enzo's arms in silence and Ayla was still upstairs
in Welton's room trying to cheer him up. The doorbell rang and
Tylisha answered the door. "Thanks, Macal for coming." She
hugged him, then let him in the house.
"Anytime. Enzo, what's up man?" Macal gave Enzo dap.
"Where's Welton?"
"In his room." Enzo answered. "Ayla is with him."
"I'll see what I can do." Macal said.
"That's all I ask." Tylisha said.
Macal and Welton, were very close. Tylisha thought if Macal,
shared his father issues with him he might have a change of heart.
Macal reached Welton's bedroom door and knocked.
"Who is it?" Welton asked.
"Uncle Macal."
Ayla walked over to answer the door, greeting her uncle, with
her beautiful, angelic smile and jumped in his arms. "Hi, Uncle
Macal!"
"Hey, baby girl!" Macal's heart always melted when his niece
brought on the charm. She reminded him so much of Tylisha. "I
need to talk to your brother alone."
"Okay." Ayla said, leaving the room.
"Hey, nephew." Macal greeted, giving Welton a manly hug.
"Hey, Uncle Macal."
"Your momma called and said something was bothering you."
Macal took a seat next to Welton. "Wanna talk to your Unc about
it?"
"It's my so called, dad." Welton rolled his eyes. "After all this
time he wants to come back."
"How do you feel about that?"
"He walked out on us like it was the easiest thing to do." Welton
said. "Even when he was around all he ever did was hurt momma.

Jamila

It broke my heart seeing her cry all the time. She tried to hide it, but I saw her. When Enzo came along things got better. Momma is happier than she's ever been. Amery is cool. Ligia and Vax are nice. Now he wants to come back when things are good. I don't think so."

Macal sat in silence listening to Welton's plight.

"You know momma. She tries to act like everything is okay and that she was okay, but I knew the truth. I knew everything was not okay and she was not okay."

Macal nodded in agreement. He knew Tylisha played tough to hide her hurt. Hearing Welton talk about Tylisha and Milton, took Macal back to a familiar place. "I understand you wanna protect your mother. I know you love her and it tore you up inside, because you couldn't do anything to take her pain away."

"That's right." Welton said.

"I felt the exact same way about my momma."

Welton turned to face Macal. "You did?"

"Yes, I did." Macal said. "My dad did things that made my momma cry, too. I felt helpless seeing her in pain, knowing there was nothing I could do about it."

"Did you hate your dad, too?" Welton asked.

"Still do." Macal confessed. "But unlike me you have a chance."

"A chance to do what?"

"A chance to tell your father how you feel." Macal said. "I never got a chance to confront my father about his wrongdoings, before he died, and how it affected me and our family. You can tell your dad exactly how you feel. Ask him all the questions you want. If he really cares about you and wanna make things right, he'll listen. After everything is said and done, you can decide if you wanna start fresh and build a relationship with him."

Welton let his uncle's words marinate for a brief moment. "I feel what you saying but I'm not ready. Is it okay, if I think it over?"

"You take all the time you need." Macal pat Welton on the back and got up to walk out the door.

Macal, opened the door and Welton called out. "Hey Unc." Macal turned around and Welton said with gratitude. "Thanks."

Macal walked over to hug Welton. "That's what I'm here for."

Macal made his way downstairs, when Tylisha saw him, she jumped off the couch with anticipation. "How did it go?"

"He said he'll think about it." Macal answered.

Tylisha settled with that, wrapped herself in Macal's arms, and kissed his cheek. "Thank you so much. I don't know where I'll be without you."

"Same here, baby girl." Macal said. "Same here."

Jamila

Chapter 22

"Here's your food, baby." The female correctional officer at the DeKalb County Correctional Facility handed Jeromy a bag from Red Lobster.

"Thanks." Jeromy said, giving the C.O. a fifty-dollar bill. "Here's something for your trouble."

"Thanks." She said, putting the money in her pocket. "You need your dick wet?"

"Can't, my cellie will be back in any minute. I'll let you know where to meet me." Jeromy gave her a quick kiss.

"Alright." And the C.O. left.

Jeromy hated being locked up, but he made the best of it. Made a few contacts. Female C.O.s made sure he was straight and gave him head and pussy from time to time. He knew he was public enemy number one in the free world, but he didn't give a fuck. As far as he was concerned the world could eat a dick. He did miss his baseball career, the money, and the countless bitches on his dick that came along with it. He would forever hate, Thuy, for snatching his life from under his feet and causing his demise.

"What's up, nigga?" Jeromy's cellmate Slope made his return.

"Slope, what's up with you?"

"Found out some shit you might be interested in."

"Which is?"

"It's about your ex-baby momma."

"You gotta be way more specific." That could be any bitter bitch. Correction, any bitter bitch, Jeromy, didn't have to have killed for not staying in her fucking place.

"The one that's doing all those shows about you." Slope answered. "The one that got you here. Brown skin with the ching-chong name."

"Oh, that bitch!" Jeromy figured out he was talking about Thuy.

"Yeah her."

"What about that bitch? As if I give a fuck."

"It's not really her, it's about her new nigga."

Jeromy didn't give a fuck about, Thuy, but something about her

Jamila

giving another man the time of day and the thought of her letting him stick his dick where his used to be, fucked up his ego.

"Her what?"

"Her new nigga, bought your house and some of your shit at an auction." Slope updated. "He's gonna tear it down and build a new one on the same fucking spot. The chick bought your Ferrari and gave it away to some charity."

"That petty ass hoe." Jeromy's deep penetrated hatred for Thuy, boiled over.

First, she put him in this motherfucker. Then she goes on a woe as me tour going on all those fucking talk shows, telling their motherfucking business. Now she's fucking another nigga and talked him into buying his house and his shit. Jeromy knew, Thuy, was behind it. That's just the kind of calculating bitch she was.

"If that bitch thinks she's gonna get away with having another nigga jack my shit, she's got another motherfucking thing coming." Jeromy growled viciously.

"I might know somebody who would be interested in helping you out." Slope offered.

Jeromy calmed down, "What are you talking about?"

"It sounds to me that you and my last cellie, both hate this, Thuy, bitch."

"Who was your last cellie?"

"Her brother, Jett."

That answer made Jeromy go from pissed the fuck off to happy as fuck. He knew about Thuy's siblings and her daddy issues. Maybe he could use this to his advantage.

"Keep talking."

Addicted to the Drama 2

Chapter 23

Macal, Thuy, Tylisha, Welton and Ayla, had a full day of merriment at Zoo Atlanta. The real reason for this outing was so the kids could meet Milton. Everyone agreed that the meeting should take place in a fun, public setting in case things went wrong.

"I loved the panda exhibit." Thuy said, as the group walked around the zoo with the exception of Macal, who had to stop in the bathroom.

"Me too, Miss Thuy. They're my favorite animals." Ayla said.

"I like the tigers and lions." Welton said.

"You on your own with that." Tylisha said to Welton. "I don't wanna be anywhere near them."

"Amen to that!" Thuy agreed.

"I'll stick with the birds." Tylisha said.

"We need to see the elephants." Ayla said. "One-time Aunt Fallon took a picture of an elephant and copied it in a drawing. I still have it."

"Those elephants are amazing." Then it dawned on Thuy, that Ayla mentioned a foreign name to her. "Who is Aunt Fallon?"

"She was married to Uncle Macal." Ayla answered innocently.

Oh shit. This nigga never told this girl he was married? Tylisha thought. "Uh Welton, why don't you and your sister go watch the rock wall climbers."

"Okay momma. Let's go, Ayla." Welton took Ayla by the hand and went on their way.

"And come back within thirty minutes, so we can meet your daddy at the petting zoo." Tylisha yelled.

"Okay." The kids yelled back.

"Where the hell is that brother of mine? How long does it take to take a shit?" Soon as Tylisha said that she remembered something. *I forgot, one of his hoes work here.* She then saw the puzzled look on Thuy's face. Even though she had a good feeling why, she asked the question anyway. "Are you alright Thuy?"

"I'm good. I was thinking about the name Fallon. I've heard that name before." Thuy shared. "That was the name of that nice

107

woman, I bumped into a while back. Even though I only met her only once, I somehow felt connected to her."

"That's pretty odd, but common." Tylisha said. "I heard of people who feel connected to complete strangers."

"I'm back." Macal made himself known.

"Hey baby." Thuy leaped into Macal's arms and kissed him. She smelled an awful strange odor on him and was taken aback with disgust. "Ew, nigga your ass stank worse than the animals! When we get home your ass is going straight to the shower."

"I second that shit." Tylisha agreed as she covered her nose.

"And another thing. Who is, Fallon?" Thuy asked.

Fallon's name set off loud ass alarms in Macal's brain. "Fallon?"

"Ayla mentioned the picture Fallon drew for her." Tylisha said.

She couldn't be mad at Ayla for spilling the tea. It was a known fact that only three types of people told the truth. The intoxicated, the pissed the fuck off, and kids. Tylisha found it quite odd, that it had been almost a full year and Macal, never once mentioned this important information to Thuy.

"Ayla, said y'all used to be married." Thuy told Macal.

"Yes, Fallon is my ex-wife." Macal admitted.

"You never told me you were married." Thuy pointed out. "How come?"

"Yeah Macal, how come?" Tylisha repeated, making Macal give her dagger eyes.

Will you shut the fuck up! Macal wanted to say to his extra baby sister but knew better.

Of course, that look didn't faze Tylisha one bit.

"I told you about my last relationship before you saw it on the news." Thuy said. "Why you never told me about Fallon?"

Macal didn't really wanna talk about, Fallon. Also, how could he tell, Thuy, that he was the one in that speeding limo and what went down inside.

"My bad, baby." Macal rubbed Thuy's cheek. "It was a terrible mistake, that I would like to put behind me."

"Oh, I get it. Things ended that badly, huh?" Thuy assumed.

You don't know the half of it. Tylisha thought.

She knew Macal like a book. She knew what he was trying to pull.

"All that matters, is that we ended things, so we can both move on to happier, healthier lives." Macal dressed up his side of the story.

"That's good." Thuy said. She heard her phone ring and pulled it out of her handbag. She glanced at her caller I.D. "It's momma, I gotta take this."

"Tell her I said hi." Macal said.

"Ditto." Tylisha said.

Thuy walked away to answer the call. When she wasn't able to be seen Tylisha gave the back of Macal's head a hard smack.

"Ouch!" Macal shrieked, rubbing the back of his head. "Tylisha what the fuck was that for? With your crazy ass."

Tylisha looked around for the person, Macal, was supposed to be calling crazy, because she knew it wasn't her. "Crazy, Moi? I'm not the one who's withholding important information from my significant other. Not to mention, sneaking off to fuck a hygiene challenged hoe in the bathroom."

This girl knows me too well. "I don't know what you talking ab—"

"Nigga, cut the fucking shit!" Tylisha shut down Macal's pathetic attempt to lie. "You might be able to bullshit, Thuy, Fallon, and all your hoes. But, you can't, nor will you ever be able to bullshit your baby sister. Now why didn't you tell Thuy about Fallon?"

"Because it wasn't important." Macal simply replied.

"The hell it ain't." Tylisha insisted. "I'm guessing you also didn't tell Thuy, you were in the limo the night of her shooting either." Who the fuck was Tylisha kidding. This was Macal she was talking to. "Of course, your black ass didn't!"

"Look Tylisha, I got everything under control." Macal said, in his weak ass defense.

Is this nigga serious? "You said that shit before, but you and the hoe almost got killed in that accident, because you couldn't control your dick! Now Fallon is locked away in that mental hospital.

Jamila

Don't you see how your actions affect other people? Also, you can't do the same shit over and over again and expect different results."

"Thuy and the kids are coming this way." Macal whispered to Tylisha.

Perfect timing because this conversation was making him uneasy.

"It's about that time to meet Milton at the petting zoo." Tylisha said. Deep down she knew talking sense into Macal was like talking to a wall, but she gave it a try anyway. "Leave these hoes alone and grow the fuck up before you lose everything!"

"Okay—okay, I'll try to do better." Macal promised.

"That's better than nothing." Tylisha settled.

Chapter 24

The *Platinum Palace*, was jumping like crazy. Coming through the door was Bryn, wearing a navy blue designer suit with a matching hat, and Dolce and Gabanna sunglasses. To his left was, Vida, dressed in a lavender, strapless, jumpsuit with silver stilettos. To his right was, Thuy, wearing a black dress with sparkling, black, peek toe pumps topped off with a glittery slightly, off white faux fur coat resting on her shoulders.

All eyes were on them. The aroma of hate and jealousy, filled the club and was drawn to the trio. The women hating on, Thuy and Vida's beauty. Men hating on Bryn for having two fine, sexy, ass women on his arm. Also, the fact that he was gay pissed them off even more. The women were also pissed, that they would never have a shot at a man as fine as Bryn. He wasn't flamboyant with his homosexuality, but the subtle clues were there.

The three friends didn't give a fuck about the haterade, thrown at them. In fact, they embraced it. Their plans for the night, was to have a good time and get turnt up. Bryn had even hired a driver to make it happen. After taking over the dance floor with their moves, they enjoyed their drinks at their table.

"I haven't danced that much since college." Bryn took a sip of his drink.

"I know, you danced enough for the three of us." Thuy joked.

"We should do this more often." Vida said.

"How are things with you and Sam?" Thuy asked Vida.

"With that man, everyday seems to get better and better." Vida was glowing.

Thuy was happy for her best friend and cousin. They deserved genuine unconditional love and happiness.

"Next week he's taking me to visit his dad." Vida continued.

"Tell Uncle Sam, I said hi." Thuy said.

"To bad Tylisha and Ligia couldn't join us." Bryn said.

"I know." Thuy said. "One of Tylisha's clients wanted her to decorate their parents summer home in Hilton Head, South Carolina."

"And Ligia took Amery along to visit her mother in New Orleans." Vida said. "They were off the chain at the all-white yacht party."

"I remember." Thuy nodded.

"I don't." Bryn said.

"Of course not, dear. You spent most of the party at the bar." Vida laughed.

"Drunk ass." Thuy teased.

"Whatever bitches." Bryn threw up his two middle fingers at Thuy and Vida.

"Sorry Bryn, but we don't have dicks." Thuy sarcastically responded to Bryn with a straight face and everybody busted out laughing.

"I noticed one of those bartenders at the party was checking you out on the sly." Vida told Bryn.

"I know, but he wasn't my type." Bryn said.

"Why not?" Thuy asked.

"I don't fuck with down low niggas." Bryn answered.

Thuy and Vida were surprised. "How did you know he was on the D.L." Thuy asked.

"Shit I know." It was a sure thing to Bryn. "I saw that wedding ring blinging on his finger and him trying to get some chick's phone number."

"Damn." Thuy and Vida exclaimed.

"Uh huh." Bryn nodded. "Y'all know I ain't with that fake, secret shit."

"Right—right." Thuy and Vida agreed.

"If he'll lie to her, then he'll lie to me." Bryn concluded. "Look I'm gay and I'm not ashamed. I know some people don't agree with my lifestyle and it's cool. As long as they don't come at me wrong. At least I keep it one-hundred. It's these D.L. niggas I got a problem with. Lying to themselves, laying down with their wives and girlfriends, while fucking other niggas behind their backs. That's some foul, scandalous shit. Putting these women, themselves, and everybody else in danger, because they wanna hide who the fuck they are. Some of them try to holla at me, I tell they asses to kick rocks. Don't put me in your secret life. I'm no side nigga, if you're too ashamed to have me on your arm in public, you ain't getting this ass or dick in private. Rant over."

"Well said." Thuy applauded Bryn's rant.

"I second that." Vida joined in on the applause.

"Besides if I can come out at the tender age of thirteen during the don't ask, don't tell nineties they asses can come out in twenty-tens when it's all the way open now." Bryn said.

"You different Bryn. You were never really in the closet." Thuy said.

Bryn chuckled. "That's true, when I came out to my family during Thanksgiving dinner. All they had to say was okay and went right on eating. Dad said he and momma, knew about me before I could even spell the word gay."

"I remember you telling us that." Thuy said. "Then you said your brother and his girlfriend now wife came home late for dinner and you told them you just came out."

Vida laughed. "They high fived each other and cheered, *He finally admits it*!"

"I told momma, you came the closet a week afterwards and she was like, *What closet was that boy supposed to be in?*" Thuy laughed, "I need another drink."

"Me too." Bryn said. "I bought the last round. Whose turn is it to buy the next round?"

"It's my turn." Thuy raised her hand, getting out of her seat. "What y'all want?"

"Surprise us." Vida said.

"Got it." Thuy walked over to the bar, the bartender immediately noticed her beauty, and quickly made his way towards her.

"What can I get for you, young lady?" The bartender asked with a smile.

"What do you recommend for me and my two friends over there?" Thuy pointed at Vida and Bryn.

The bartender looked over at Vida and Bryn. *What would two beautiful sexy ladies and their faggot friend like?* "May I suggest the Scorpion Bowl?"

Jamila

"Scorpion bowl, what's that?" Thuy had never heard of such a drink and was curious to know what the hell it was.

"It's a mixture of fruit juice, rum, vodka, gin and grenadine." The bartender explained. "It's served in a volcano bowl cup, that looks like an island inside. The drink can be served individually or into a larger cup to share with your friends."

"I'll take three of them and we'll see how we like it."

"Coming right up, I'll bring them to your table."

"Excellent."

Thuy went back to the table and Vida noticed something was missing. "Where are the drinks?"

"The bartender is gonna bring them out." Thuy assured, sitting down. "He suggested the Scorpion Bowl."

"This should be good." Bryn said.

The bartender arrived with their drinks. "Here you are ladies." He handed Thuy and Vida their drinks. He gave Bryn his drink and added. "And gentleman."

"Thanks." Thuy tipped the bartender and sipped the drink. "These are great."

"Told you." The bartender smiled.

"Do you want the big bowl with the three straws?"

"Yes!" The trio answered in unity.

"And add three blue motherfuckers to my tab." Vida went ahead and took care of her round of drinks.

"Coming right up." The bartender said and took his leave.

Bryn took another sip of his drink. "Damn Thuy, you introduced us to some new shit."

"You can thank the bartender for that." Thuy took another sip.

"Mmm, I need to learn how to make these." Vida said.

After having three more drinks, Vida said. "Good thing we hired a driver tonight."

"I need to go to the bathroom." Thuy said and got out of her seat.

Thuy made her way through the crowd and found the bathroom. She was in luck, the bathroom was empty. She went into the very last stall to take a piss. While reliving herself another woman came

114

in with a terrible funk. Thuy knew it was the woman because the bathroom didn't smell like that before. Not only was this scent stank as fuck, but it was also familiar.

Thuy got out of the stall to wash her hands and check her hair and makeup. The stank chick got out of the stall and washed her hands. She was a pretty-light skinned woman but needed to check her body odor or improve her taste in perfume.

Thuy's hair and makeup check were interrupted by another woman busting in the bathroom yelling. "Fucking bitch."

Thuy turned around and saw the woman slap the hell out of stank light-skin.

"Oh shit!" Thuy yelled.

The women began to tussle and exchange blows. Thuy just stood there in disbelief.

"Nasty stank ass, hoe!" The woman punched stank light-skin in the face and stank light-skin wrapped her hands around the woman's neck.

If the women weren't blocking, Thuy's path to the door she would've let these silly bitches knock each other's brains out. Since she needed to get out, she had no choice, but to try and play peace-maker.

"Ladies stop it, break it up!" Thuy ordered and pulled stank light-skin off the woman who was taking hard punches to the eye and jaw.

"You better stay the fuck away from Macal bitch!" The woman yelled at stank light-skin.

"Macal!" Thuy turned around to the woman stank light-skin was tearing apart and recognized her immediately. "Wait a minute! You're that bitch who tried to knock me down in New Orleans. And you the same chick that rolled up on me and my man at the park." Stank light-skin left in a hurry. "Who the fuck are you?" Thuy rudely asked the woman.

"Thuy Ellis, nice to meet you." The bitch greeted smugly.

This bitch knows my motherfucking name. "Bitch I asked you a question. Who the fuck are you and how the fuck do you know my man?" Thuy interrogated.

"You need to ask him." The thot responded.

"No, I'm asking your ass bitch." Thuy wanted answers, she wanted them right motherfucking now. "If you don't want another ass whooping, I suggest you answer my motherfucking question. *This hoe don't know who the fuck she's dealing with.*

"What question you want me to answer dear? You asked two of them." She replied with cocky sarcasm.

And this bitch is trying my motherfucking gangsta. "Don't fucking play with me. I'm actually being nice about this shit, but you fucking with the wrong one!" Thuy hissed. She was in no mood for this hoe's smart aleck remarks. "I'm gonna ask you this one motherfucking time and your hoe ass better answer me. Who the fuck are you and how do you know my man?"

"My name is Lolette Bates, me and your man Macal, have been fucking for some time before you showed up. Actually, we never really stopped." She giggled.

Not this shit again. Thuy, thought she'd never have to worry about side bitches ever again.

She'd deal with Macal, later but first she had to check this bitch. What she just told her, fucked her up, but she wasn't gonna let this thot trip her up.

"If that's true your ass is gonna stop fucking him today, because he's my man now bitch! And if I catch your nasty hoe ass anywhere near mine, your ass is gonna end up dusted up in here." Thuy warned.

Lolette, let out a taunting laugh and went in for the kill. "Where the fuck was this big bad talk when you got that ass shot up? By the way how's your son Day'zon?"

Lolette's words caused, Thuy, to shake her head and cover her face with her hands. "My baby, my baby!" She sobbed.

Lolette, smiled with victory, enjoying the sight of Thuy crumbling. "Yeah bitch! You ain't hard. You ain't shit! All that shit you was talking and got no motherfucking bite."

Thuy continued to bawl uncontrollably with severe emotion as Lolette continued to taunt her.

Addicted to the Drama 2

Lolette, decided to take it up a notch by leaning in her ear and whispering. "If you was fucking your men right. You wouldn't have to worry about nigga's trying to kill your ass, then running to a bitch like me who knows how to fu—"

Thuy turned around with light speed and whipped out the strongest, most powerful, sucker punch to Lolette's face knocking her out, on her ass.

Thuy looked in the mirror, there was no trace of her crying on her face. She silently patted herself on the back for the Academy Award winning performance she'd put on. She quickly checked her appearance and made the necessary adjustments, to make sure she looked flawless.

Cool and calmly Thuy stepped over a still knocked out Lolette and walked out of the bathroom like the boss bitch she was and found her friends.

"Guys let's call it a night. I'm tired." Thuy said.

"Good idea." Vida agreed.

The trio walked out the club and entered the black Hummer limo. "Where to?" The driver asked.

"Home." Vida answered.

"Home." Bryn mirrored Vida's answer.

"Alright home it is then." The driver said.

"Not me." Thuy interjected. "I need you to drop me off at my boyfriend's penthouse." *Because that nigga got some motherfucking explaining to do.* Thuy thought before giving the driver the directions.

Jamila

Chapter 25

"I win again!" Macal cheered in triumph, collecting his poker winnings from Enzo and Vax, in the dining room of his penthouse.

"Damn it Macal, you're killing us!" Enzo whined.

"I know right. If I keep losing like this, I'm gonna have to return Ligia's gift for a refund." Vax joked.

"What did you get her?" Macal asked, shuffling the cards.

Vax pulled a jewelry box out of his pocket and opened it revealing a pair of beautiful, eighteen carats, white gold diamond earrings. "Check it out."

"Shit. Those earrings are blinding me!" Macal was in awe.

"They are breathtaking. What's the occasion?" Enzo asked curiously. "It can't be Ligia's birthday. That was last month."

"Ligia was named Principal of the Year and this is like a congratulatory gift. I'm gonna give these to her, so she can wear them for the awards banquet next week." Vax said.

"They gave it to the right person." Enzo said. "Ligia is very dedicated to her students."

"Y'all ready to play another hand?" Macal asked.

"I'm ready, I need to win something." Vax said.

The cards were dealt, and the guys looked over their hands. They were completely silent in deep concentration.

Boom! The guys literally jumped out of their skins when they heard the door slam. They looked up and saw a highly pissed off Thuy marching towards the table.

"Macal we need to talk right now!" She demanded.

"Thuy, what the hell?" Macal didn't know what the fuck was going on with Thuy. She'd never acted like this before. "Girl, you need to calm your ass down! Can't you see I have guests?"

"Guests? These niggas ain't nobody. It's just Enzo and Vax." Thuy dismissed. "She glanced over at the two, "No offense, hey y'all."

"Hey." Enzo and Vax greeted.

Thuy turned her fury back on Macal. "Nigga we need to talk right motherfucking now!"

Jamila

"Thuy, with all due respect, but whatever the problem is can it wait until this hand is over." Vax politely requested. "I've been losing all night."

"Humph!" Thuy casually walked around the table to take a peek over Macal's shoulder to see his cards. "Royal Flush."

"Fuck." Vax threw his cards on the table in defeat.

"We'll catch y'all later." Enzo said, following Vax on the way out the door.

"Goodnight." Macal said.

"Bye!" Thuy bid Enzo and Vax farewell, closed the door behind them, and locked it.

"Bet you she found out about Lolette." Enzo whispered to Vax.

"That'll be the only bet I'd win tonight." Vax joked in a serious tone.

He and Enzo shared a laugh as they left the building.

"Girl why the hell did you bust up my poker game like that?" Macal, wanted to know what this chick's problem was.

"Lolette Bates?" Was, Thuy's only reply.

Oh shit! "Huh?"

"Nigga your motherfucking ass heard me!" Thuy rolled up on Macal, getting in his face. "When I was at the club, I had to use the bathroom. Before I could leave Lolette and another bitch started fighting blocking my way. Now that I think about it that smelly bitch Lolette, was fighting smelled a lot like your ass did when you came back from the bathroom at the zoo. I remembered her face too. She got locked in that cage last year. Those hoes were fighting over a nigga named Macal."

"It must've been some other nigga na—"

Thuy put an end to Macal's lying, by slapping the shit out of him. "Nigga don't motherfucking play with me! Unlike that smelly bitch, that Lolette hoe was dumb enough to try me. She said y'all been fucking for a long motherfucking time and y'all never stopped. I know it's the same bitch, that rolled up on us at the park, and tried to knock me down in New Orleans."

"Baby, I'm sorry." Was all Macal could say. He was cold busted.

120

Addicted to the Drama 2

"Don't be sorry, nigga. Answer my damn question. Who the fuck is this bitch?"

Macal sighed and made an attempt to dress it up a bit. Most people would call it a half-truth, leaving out important information, or boldface lying. Macal would prefer to call it saving his ass.

"Alright, I confess. Lolette and I did have a thing going on, but it's over. She's having a hard time letting go."

"Well that bitch gonna learn today." Thuy snapped. "After that stank zoo bitch, beat her ass, I had to lay the hoe out myself. That'll teach that bitch not to throw my shooting and Day'zon in my motherfucking face."

Macal was appalled by what he'd just heard. "She did what?"

"Yes, the fuck she did." Thuy lashed out, letting the tears flow freely.

It took everything she had not to shed a tear back at the club. She didn't wanna give that hoe the satisfaction of breaking in front of her.

"That bitch went there, and I had to show her ass what time it was." Thuy barked.

Macal remembered the pain, Thuy, felt when they were in the hospital together. Thuy was beyond devastated. "Baby, I'm sorry!"

Macal tried to pull Thuy in his arms, but she pushed him away. "Don't be sorry, nigga, be careful. I don't know how Fallon dealt with this type of fuckery, but I ain't the one. I don't play that shit!" Thuy sighed and kept going. "I'm gonna spare you the agony of admitting, that nasty ass rainbow thong belongs to Lolette and that you snuck off to fuck that stank, zoo bitch. Nigga, this ain't a game!"

Macal was sick and tired of hearing Thuy go on and on about this. He didn't wanna talk about it anymore. Macal lifted Thuy in the air and threw her over his shoulder.

"What the fuck are you doing?" Thuy screamed. "Nigga put me down, right now! We ain't finished talking about this shit!"

Oh, yes we are! Macal thought, smiling as he carried Thuy upstairs, into the bedroom.

"Your ass ain't gonna have these hoes disrespecting me!" Thuy

121

continued to yell.

Macal laid her flat on her back on the bed.

"Nigga I ain't playing with your motherfucking ass!" Thuy yelled.

Macal reached under Thuy's dress to take off her black thong.

"Nigga I'm serious!" Thuy protested.

Macal then threw her legs over his shoulders and smashed his head between her thighs. He stuck out his tongue and licked her clit.

"Nigga I'm ser—ah!" Thuy moaned. "I'm not gonna—oh—"

Macal whipping her clit with his tongue, was making it very difficult to concentrate, and think clearly.

"Oh shit!" Thuy came when Macal sucked hard on the clit. Her legs started to shake. Then she felt Macal's two fingers inside her moistened pussy. He did a circular motion deep inside, as he continued to make her clit swell with his mouth.

Thuy's body trembled with extreme sexual gratification. Her mouth couldn't form complete words.

Macal looked up at Thuy's dazed face, smiling. He got on his feet and pulled his dick out. He began stroking his yardstick nice and slow, before climbing on top of Thuy, and sliding his dick deep inside her sweet wetness. Macal and Thuy, rolled all over the bed with their genitals intertwined and their tongues tied up in knots.

The sex was very intoxicating. Deep down Thuy, knew she should still be pissed at Macal and the discovery of his transgressions, but having his dick deep inside her, making her bust countless nuts, was making it easy for her to get over it.

Thuy had to admit, the sad and insane truth. Unlike Jeromy, Macal could fuck his way out of it. If any slut, bitch, and thot out there thinks her man and dick is up for grabs, they had another motherfucking thing coming. There was a new H.B.I.C. in town and her name was Thuy Mackenzie Ellis. These hoes better move the fuck back, because underneath the sophistication and refinement, lied a gangsta bitch ready to strike if fucked with!

Chapter 26

"You are quite the little artist." Fallon complimented Ayla's drawing of a panda, while they were sitting in the visiting room of Wadley Hospital.

"Thanks, Aunt Fallon." Ayla said, giving Fallon a hug.

"Welton how's school?" Fallon asked.

"Great!" Welton answered. "Next week my school is going on a field trip, thanks for the book."

"Anytime." Fallon said. "I know how much you like to read."

"Kids I need to talk to Aunt Fallon in private. Y'all go over there and watch T.V." Tylisha instructed, pointing at the T.V.

"Yes, momma." Welton said.

He and Ayla went over to the couch to watch T.V.

"How you been?" Tylisha asked Fallon, taking a seat at the table.

"Pretty good." Fallon nodded. "Aunt Naomi introduced me to her new boyfriend, Park."

"She's dating again? Good for her."

"He seems like a nice guy. How are things with Enzo?"

"Wonderful as usual." Tylisha handed Fallon a shopping bag. "I got you something, while I passed through Savannah, during my Hilton Head assignment."

Fallon dug in the bag and pulled out the contents in the bag. "Art supplies with a carrying case engraved with my name on it. Thanks!" Fallon gave Tylisha a hug.

"Anytime."

"I got, Grandma Doris' letter yesterday." Fallon said. "She said she and Gladys are going to Las Vegas."

"They love themselves some casinos." Tylisha giggled.

Fallon sighed before asking the hard question. "How's Macal?"

"He's making it." Tylisha struggled to find an honest answer. Saying that Macal was doing pretty good or okay would be a bold-face lie in her book.

"How is his girlfriend?"

Tylisha was about to say something but Fallon stopped her. "It's okay. I know he's dating again."

"How did you know?"

Fallon shrugged. "Call it a hunch. A sixth sense and I dragged it out of Aunt Naomi."

"I'm sorry you had to learn that." Tylisha sympathized.

"It was bound to happen. She's probably a much better woman than I'll ever be." Fallon said in defeat.

"You shouldn't say things like that." Tylisha shook her head. "You're a good woman."

"Who tried to kill her cheating husband and so called, slut, best friend and locked in a nuthouse as a result." Fallon reminded.

"Fallon you were betrayed and hurt. You weren't in your right mind. I understand, everyone has a breaking point."

"My breaking point cost me my marriage." Fallon said. "I still haven't heard from or seen Macal. He must really hate me."

Macal needs to talk to this girl! "He doesn't hate you. It's just difficult for him to face things." Tylisha tried to explain. "You know that."

Fallon nodded in agreement, recalling the guilt Macal carried with him about his mother's death.

"The fucked-up part is with my relationship history Macal, is the best man I ever had. Even though he did me extremely dirty at least he never hit me, called me out of my name, or did what the bastard before him did."

Tylisha became curious. "What did the bastard do?"

"It's too painful to talk about." The memories of the incident were too much for Fallon to bear.

"Understood." Tylisha dropped the subject.

Whatever this asshole did Tylisha could see it left Fallon seriously damaged. Unbeknownst to Macal he made the damage stick.

"I saw a rerun of this talk show episode the other day." Fallon shared. "They had this woman on there who went through a serious ordeal. Her story was very heartbreaking and powerful and that's saying something coming from me. It's amazing how she fought so hard to stay alive. The baby she was carrying didn't make it."

"You don't say." Tylisha said with interest.

"The thing is we met before."

"You met this woman?"

"Yeah." Fallon's face lit up when she talked about the woman. "It was the night I lost the baby. I ran into her at Lullaby Deluxe. She was so excited about being a mom. She couldn't wait for her son to be born. I felt some type of strong connection to her."

What the fuck? It can't be. "What was the woman's name?" Tylisha needed to be sure.

"Thuy Ellis." Fallon answered. "Her ex-fiancé was that baseball player, who put a hit out on her, and their unborn son."

Oh fuck. Macal is dating a woman who by chance met his now ex-wife and these women share an unexplainable bond. Not to mention Fallon almost ran Thuy off the road before she was shot. Tylisha didn't know what to do with this new information. She had to get the fuck out of there and wrap her head around this shit.

"I better hit the road. You take care of yourself." Tylisha prepared to leave and summoned her children. "Kids it's time to go, say goodbye to Aunt Fallon."

"Goodbye, Aunt Fallon." Welton and Ayla gave Fallon a big hug.

"Goodbye, babies stay sweet." Fallon said. She gave Tylisha a hug and added. "Goodbye, thanks for everything."

"Anytime." Tylisha said.

Jamila

Chapter 27

Today Ligia was feeling a lot better health wise. She treated herself by taking a trip to Victoria's Secret and found a candy apple, red, lingerie outfit that fit like a second skin on her body.

In the bathroom she tried on her new bright red lipstick and touched up her makeup. She admired her beautician's handiwork with her tight curls. She took one last look on the mirror making sure she was looking sexy for her husband when he arrived home.

She put on her matching robe and exited the bathroom. Vax walked in the bedroom, closing the door behind him. He took off his jacket and placed his briefcase on the floor in annoyance.

"Hey baby." Ligia walked over to Vax and gave him a smooch. "Rough day?"

"You can say that." Vax sighed, sitting on the bed. "We had an emergency meeting, because we found out one of our store managers was stealing. The shit was a mess."

"Sealing?" Ligia was appalled and positioned herself behind Vax massaging his shoulders, to calm his nerves.

"Yes stealing." Vax reiterated. "At the same store, Thuy's mother used to run. That woman had that place running like clockwork. I should've known something was wrong. How could I've been so blind?"

Vax took pride in his family's business, that was built with his father's bare hands. Thuy's grandmother ran their very first store and helped make it into a big success. When Vax was ten his father died, and his mother took over the business. At first there was skepticism, because she was a housewife, who never held a job, that earned a paycheck in her life. She proved her doubters wrong by bringing the company to nationwide success. She learned fast by watching her husband and taking notes.

Vax never regretted ending his music career to take over the business when his mother died. His parents always taught him to treat everyone with respect, but don't be a fool. He always made sure his employees and customers were taken care of. That's why the theft was really fucking with him.

Jamila

"Don't blame yourself, baby." Ligia tried to cheer Vax up while working her massaging techniques from his shoulders to his back. "That's on her not you. You are a brilliant businessman."

Vax turned around and rubbed Ligia's cheek. "Thanks sweetheart." He said with gratitude. "How was your day?"

Ligia sighed. "I had to go shopping to take my mind off the crazy day I had. I had to stop a food fight."

"Food fight?"

"Yep. I had to put my favorite suit in the cleaners and get my hair done. Mashed potatoes landed on my back. Green peas on my sleeve. Some corn got in my hair." The food fight story made Vax laugh like a hyena. "Quit laughing, it ain't funny!"

"Yes, it is." Vax kept on laughing. "Come on, have some humor about yourself."

"Alright, alright." Ligia nodded, getting off the bed. "Since you wanna laugh at my expense you can forget about this." She let her robe drop to the floor to show off her new lingerie.

Vax's mouth watered at the sight of his wife's sexy body popping out of the well-designed ball of string. "Oh, no baby, I'll be good!"

"Just think. You were on my mind when I saw this at Victoria's Secret." Ligia let Vax take a good look at how her attire was doing a terrible job covering her ass and the nipples of her titts.

"You really gonna do me like that?"

"You know damn well I'm not punishing myself like that." Ligia climbed on top of Vax and stuck her tongue in his mouth.

She slowly undressed him until his sexy muscular body was completely exposed and his long hard dick jumped for joy.

"This is so unfair." Vax playfully pouted.

"What's so unfair baby?"

"I'm all naked and you're still dressed."

Ligia giggled. "You're right, that is unfair." She slipped out of her sexy getup. "Feel better?"

"Not yet." Vax laid Ligia flat on her back and pressed his body on top of hers.

He pushed both of her legs back and shoved his dick deep inside

128

her pussy.

"Now I feel better." Without another word he grabbed one of Ligia's titties and sucked hard. His long hard strokes made Ligia scream out his name with intense pleasure.

Her pussy was smothering the dick making it nice and wet. "Ah!" Ligia's moans motivated Vax to keep up his stroke game.

Making Ligia moan and cum was Vax's favorite pastime. He loved the sensational feeling of her nutting on his dick and the residue from her dripping, wet pussy covering his dick, and leaking on his balls.

"Oh shit!" Ligia busted another fat nut.

She learned a long time ago from her first time making love to Vax, to never underestimate his get down in bed, because he was a generation or two older.

These young dudes need to take notes! Ligia looked straight into Vax's eyes and moaned. "I love you!"

"I love you too, baby girl!" He grunted.

Vax hit her spot hard making her scream at the top of her lungs. "Oh shit, Vax—ah!"

"Girl, you know Amery heard that."

"He'll get over it!" Ligia dismissed and concentrated on busting her next nut.

****

"Oh baby, make me cum again!"

"Shit baby, this pussy is good!"

"Ew." Amery shivered with disgust.

That did it for him. He couldn't tolerate it anymore. Playing video games and watching T.V. didn't help at all. Visiting his dad's house wasn't any better when Tylisha spent nights. Amery grabbed his iPhone and left his room.

Amery was happy to have parents who got along, and found good people who loved, and cared about them, but he could do without being subjected to getting an earful of their sex lives. He retreated to the studio, where he didn't have to hear that disgust carrying on.

Amery closed the door behind him and sighed with relief. "Peace and quiet!"

He took a seat at the piano, played, and sung along to Ben by Michael Jackson. His piano playing was interrupted by a phone call.

"Hello." Amery answered.

"Amery." Welton's voice replied.

"Welton, is this you?" Amery guessed.

"Yes. Me and Ayla are here." Welton answered.

"What's up?"

"We're stuck."

"Stuck where?"

"We're in front of some house and dad is sleep at the wheel." Welton reported.

Shit! Amery shook his head. "Where's your mom?"

"Your dad took her to some concert out of town."

"Oh yeah." Amery kicked himself for forgetting. "What about your uncle and his girlfriend?" He suggested.

"I can't get a hold of them. I don't think it's a good idea though. I don't think Uncle Macal, likes dad very much." Welton said.

"I see." Amery didn't know what to do to save his friends.

He would get his mom and Vax, but they were preoccupied.

Then he had an idea. It was crazy, but there was no choice. "Y'all in the car, right?"

"Yeah." Ayla answered.

"Hey, baby girl!" Amery greeted with a smile.

"I'm scared, Amery." Ayla sounded terrified.

"Don't be scared, baby girl. Welton and I are gonna get y'all home safe okay." Amery assured.

"Welton, is the car on the street facing the right side of the road?" Amery asked.

Welton doubled checked before giving his answer. "Yes."

hope this works. "This is what I need y'all to do. Put me on FaceTime."

Welton did as instructed and he saw Amery's face on the screen.

"Let me see your dad."

Addicted to the Drama 2

Welton brought the phone close to Milton's face. *That nigga ain't sleep. His ass is high as fuck.* Amery concluded when he saw white powder in his nostrils and his eyes rolled back.

"Have me facing the road. Does Milton have any sunglasses in the car?"

Ayla found a pair of sunglasses in the glove compartment. "Yes."

"Put them on him." Amery instructed.

"Welton I need you to get in the driver's seat and make sure nobody sees you. Ayla make sure you got that phone steady, so I can see the road."

"Amery, what are you gonna do?" Ayla asked.

"I'm gonna help y'all get home." Amery answered. "Welton I'm gonna talk you through driving home."

"That's crazy!" Welton shrieked.

"I don't see any other way." Amery shrugged his shoulders. He gave Welton a quick explanation on how to control the car and its functions. "Do you know your dad's address?"

Ayla dug in Milton's pocket for his wallet looking for his driver's license. She remembered seeing their address on her mother's license one time. "I got it."

"Good girl, let me see it."

Ayla waved the driver's license over the phone screen.

Amery looked it up on Google Maps. "Okay I got the directions. Now do exactly as I say and everything will be fine."

"Okay." Welton said.

"Alright let's go. Ayla make sure you keep that phone steady, so I can see where we're going and Welton make sure nobody can see you driving." Amery said.

"Okay." Welton and Amery said.

Fortunately for the kids the drive back to Milton's condo wasn't far. They only had to make three turns. The drive was about thirty minutes. Good thing they didn't see any cops. Luck was on their side. Amery was a pretty good teacher and Welton was a fast learner. With Amery's direction it would appear as though if Welton had over twenty-five years of driving experience. When they

131

reached the condo Welton parked the car in the driveway and got out of the driver's seat.

"Thank God, we made it." Welton breathed out in relief and hugged Ayla nice and tight.

"Shit, my head." Milton woke up from his cocaine induced daze. He looked around in disbelief. "How did we get here? Kids are you, okay?" He didn't know what the fuck happened.

The last thing he remembered, he took the kids to the arcade, and on the way back he made a quick stop to score some coke. He didn't realize how strong it was, but it was some good shit.

"You drove home." Welton lied. "You had a headache and closed your eyes for a minute."

"I did?" Milton's head was still throbbing.

"Yep." Welton and Ayla stuck with the lie.

"Oh okay." Milton accepted. "Alright kids let's go inside and play this new video game."

"Yay!" The kids cheered.

They stayed just a few feet behind Milton. They still had his phone and Amery was still on the line.

Those two are quick on their feet! Amery admired.

"That was fun!" Ayla cheered.

"Yeah, I know, but be quiet about it." Welton whispered.

"Okay." Ayla whispered. "Thanks Amery."

"Anytime." Amery said.

With all the excitement, Welton neglected to point out something until now. "We appreciate the help Amery, but I gotta know. Where did you learn how to drive?"

"My stepsister Quinn's husband, Rex. Corporate attorney by day, Car auctioneer on the side. "Amery answered with a wink and an index finger to his lips.

"Gotcha." Welton and Ayla noted that their lips are sealed about the crazy ass rescue mission.

Chapter 28

"Hey baby boy, it's momma." Thuy stood over Day'zon's grave holding a jersey wearing teddy bear in her hand. "I got you another teddy bear." She placed it on the grave. "Not a day goes by, that I don't wish you were here with me. I love you, baby boy." She was getting teary eyed and wiped them away with the back of her hand. "I'm sorry baby. I'm sorry, I couldn't save you. I did everything I could to save you. I really did!"

"Thuy!"

Thuy turned around to see who was calling her. "Tori?"

"Your secretary said you were here." Tori said.

"Yeah, I haven't been here in a while and wanted to be alone." Thuy said with gloom.

"I'm sorry." Tori apologized.

"It's okay." Thuy hugged her. "Thanks for being here."

"How are you holding up?" Tori asked with concern.

"Pretty well. How are you?"

"Great, just came back from visiting the kids." Tori decided to let her children's fathers have physical custody of the kids.

"How they, doing?"

"Good."

"I better get going." Thuy said. "I'm supposed to meet Macal at his office." Thuy said. "It was good seeing you."

"You too, I love you." Tori pulled Thuy into a big hug and kissed her on the cheek.

"I love you, too."

****

"Hey baby!" Thuy greeted Macal when she let herself in his office. "You said you wanted to see me about something?"

"Yes, I do." Macal said. He got out of his chair and handed Thuy a folder. "I had this idea, I would like your input."

"I'll see what I can do for you." Thuy grabbed the folder and skimmed through documents. It was a business plan. "You wanna put together a division that helps inspiring business owners?"

"Yep." Macal answered. "This division will also help people with newly acquired fortunes to help them manage their money wisely. From people who won the lottery to—"

"Pro athletes." Thuy finished. "You came up with this idea from our conversation?"

"Yes, I did. You gave me some great ideas. That's why I want you to help me build this division." Macal proposed.

"Me, become your business partner?" This was unbelievable to Thuy.

"Who better than you." Macal said. "You're running two businesses successfully. Your tip about the Jeromy auction was genius and you gave me this idea. Baby you're perfect for this business partnership."

"I'm very flattered." Thuy blushed, then switched to her Sheneneh from Martin impersonation. "I don't know. Let me think about it." She turned away from Macal and mumbled out loud to herself. "Are you sure? Alright." She turned back to Macal to give him her decision in her regular voice with a smile. "Sure honey."

"That's my silly baby." Macal cheered and kissed Thuy. He called his assistant and said. "Janice, hold my calls for the rest of the day." He dashed over to his minibar to grab a bottle of champagne and two glasses.

"What are you doing?" Thuy giggled.

"Grabbing this champagne and taking my woman and now business partner, to the nearest five-star hotel to celebrate." Macal rubbed Thuy's ass.

"Sounds good to me." Thuy could feel her clit throbbing through her thong thinking about what was in store for her.

Locked away in a luxury suite with her man, the finest champagne, with his dick buried all up in her pussy. What a great way to spend the rest of the day!

Addicted to the Drama 2

Chapter 29

2007
Columbus, Georgia

Fallon was sound asleep, in bed in the apartment she shared with her boyfriend Randy. She was awakened by a stiff dick rubbing up against her ass and having her nipples played with. Her panties got wet instantly.

She giggled at Randy trying to get some late-night pussy. What the hell? She's up now. Might as well give her man a treat.

"Awe baby. You don't have to play! You know you can have this pussy." She turned over to face her man.

"My pleasure."

Fallon's eyes widened with terror, when she saw that the man lying beside her, fondling her was not Randy.

"Nick! What the fuck are you doing here? Where is Randy" Fallon jumped out of bed in a panic.

"Don't worry about that. Let me get some." Nick climbed out of bed making his way towards Fallon.

"Nigga are you crazy? Randy is your brother, I'm his girl-friend. Get the fuck out of my room. Now!" She yelled.

"I will after I tear this pussy up." Nick pulled Fallon into his arms with force.

Fallon struggled her way out of Nick's arms. "If your ass ain't gonna leave, I will!"

Fallon was about to reach the door, but Nick grabbed her wrist. "Calm down and get back in bed."

"Let me go!" Fallon yelled.

When she couldn't get loose from Nick's tight grip, she kicked him in the shin, and bolted out the room. She tried to reach the front door, but Nick caught up with her, and pulled her hair.

"Bitch!" He yelled in her face and punched her.

She hit the floor hard. She tried to get up, but Nick kicked her in the ribs and pinned her down.

"Nick let me go!" Fallon screamed, struggling to get free.

Jamila

"What the fuck are you doing?" Nick reached under her nightshirt to rip her panties off. "Somebody please help me!"

Nick pulled his dick out and forced Fallon's legs open, roughly entering her. "Ah—ah!" He moaned as he roughly penetrated Fallon. Stretching her pussy beyond its limits.

"Nick please stop! You're hurting me!" Fallon begged for mercy.

Nick wrapped his hands around Fallon's throat and hissed. "Bitch shut the fuck up and take this dick."

Fallon tried to fight him off and scream, but her windpipe was closing. Plus, her strength was leaving her body. All she could do was cry and take the pain, hoping that it wouldn't take Nick long to be done. It took Nick five minutes to empty his ball sack inside Fallon.

Nick was exhausted, he needed that nut. He'd heard how Fallon was in bed and needed to see for himself. It took a few blows to get her to give in, but it was worth it.

Fallon laid there motionless, in humiliation, and disgust. The bastard actually enjoyed raping his brother's girlfriend like it was consensual sex. She didn't know what to do or say. Nick was still on top of her, with his now limp dick wedged in her now violated pussy.

Fallon felt Nick get hard again. That meant the torture was going to resume. She braced herself for another round of being raped.

Nick kissed Fallon on the lips. "Shit girl. You're a good fuck!" He lifted her right leg up and said. "Now let's tear this pussy up some more."

Nick got five violent strokes in when someone outside the door was heard yelling.

"Police!"

Boom! The door was knocked down. Four cops rushed inside the apartment.

"Get off her now!" One of the cops yelled, pulling Nick off Fallon.

A female cop saw the condition Fallon was in and helped her on the couch. "Ma'am what happened?"

"He just raped me." Fallon whimpered.

"You're under arrest!" The officer yelled and slapped the handcuffs on Nick.

"Call an ambulance, hurry!" The female cop who was tending to Fallon yelled.

Fallon was thankful the police arrived, but who'd called them, if she didn't? "How did you know?"

"Your friend, who lives across the hall, heard a disturbance and called 911." The female cop answered.

Lolette entered the apartment during the commotion. "Fallon!" She rushed to her.

"Lolette!" Fallon collapsed in her arms.

"What happened?" Lolette asked with concern.

"Nick raped me." Fallon admitted with shame.

"I'm so sorry." Lolette held Fallon tighter for protection.

The police were about to carry Nick out. Lolette marched over to Nick and gave him the biggest wad of spit to the face, she could muster up.

"Take that you bitch ass fuck nigga!" And I just came back from sucking and fucking the landlord and his brother. Lolette smiled at the thought of traces of two different types of semen were now on the filthy bastard's face.

"Y'all gonna let this bitch get away with that?" Nick complained to the cops.

Another cop got in his face and said. "Compared to what's gonna happen to you in the near future she's being lenient." He turned to his colleagues. "Get this sick bastard the fuck out of my sight."

As Nick was being carried out, the paramedics arrived with a stretcher. "Let's get you in the ambulance.

"Can I ride with her?" Lolette asked.

"Of course." the paramedic answered.

Fallon was being carried out of the apartment, with Lolette, and the female cop in tow.

Randy was seen running towards Fallon and started asking a shitload of questions. "Fallon what the fuck is going on? Why the fuck is Nick being taken away in handcuffs?"

Jamila

"This is your apartment?" The female cop asked.

"Yes, this is my apartment." Randy answered. "That's my woman on that stretcher and my brother y'all arrested. What the fuck is going on?"

Lolette went ahead and told it all. She was highly pissed. "Your nasty ass brother just raped my home girl. When I heard her scream for help I called the po-po's on his ass!"

Something didn't quite set right with Lolette and she felt she needed to address it. "I got a question. Where the fuck your ass was at this whole motherfucking time?"

"That's actually a good question, sir." The female cop agreed.

"That's a very good question." Fallon was wondering the same thing. "Randy, where did you disappear to at this late hour, while your brother was raping me?"

*****

Fallon laid wide awake, in her bed, thinking about the events of that horrible night and what followed. She was so happy to learn that Nick was stabbed to death while awaiting trial. She and Lolette, had actually gone out to celebrate. The celebration was short lived when she learned heartbreaking information behind her rape.

Fallon heard the door open and sat up. One of the workers came in with a beautiful, dark-skinned young woman, who looked like she wasn't even twenty years old yet. Fallon knew she had to be at least eighteen because this was the adult building at Wadley.

"Hey Fallon. Say hello to your new roommate." The worker said.

"My new roommate." Fallon was used to her own space, but she didn't see the problem with having a roommate. Not like she had a choice.

The worker made the introduction. "Rita Austin, this is Fallon Potter-Kilborn. I'll let you ladies get acquainted.

When they were left alone, Fallon stood in silence. Rita didn't say a word.

Fallon slowly approached Rita and extended her hand. "Hi, I'm

138

Fallon. Nice to meet you." Rita didn't say anything back. She just stared at Fallon's hand like she didn't know what to do. "It's alright. I'm not gonna hurt you."

Out of nowhere Rita burst into tears. Fallon caught her before she fell to the floor. Fallon helped Rita into her bed and let this broken young woman cry in her arms. She didn't know what this girl's problem was, but she felt her pain.

"I know baby. It's okay baby, I'm here."

Jamila

Chapter 30

The Restart Project Charity Concert was a big success. The board members decided to make the event family oriented, for the children to enjoy. The performers put on an excellent show. The survivors' testimonies were powerful. Backstage at the Lakewood Amphitheater, were Thuy and the crew. For them it was work, but they enjoyed themselves at the same time.

"How much money did we raise?" Thuy asked Bryn, who was calculating the funds on the laptop.

"Counting ticket sales, donations, and pledges we raised twenty-five million dollars and counting." Bryn answered.

"Make that thirty million dollars and counting." Macal handed Bryn an envelope with his five-million-dollar donation check.

"Thanks, Macal." Bryn said.

"Anything for the cause." Macal said and wrapped his arms around Thuy. "You guys are amazing putting all of this together."

"Don't forget the chick who decorated for this event." Tylisha said as she walked towards them.

"Awe Tylisha nobody's forgetting about you." Macal hugged his baby sister.

"Uh huh." Tylisha said. "I can't wait for Ligia's performance."

"Me neither." Thuy said and saw Marsha on the arm of a good looking bronzed skinned man coming their way. "Marsha are you ready?"

"Yes I am." Marsha answered.

"And who is this?" Thuy asked referring to Marsha's companion.

Marsha giggled. "Everybody this is my man, Zack."

You go girl. Thuy thought. "How did y'all meet?"

Marsha and Zack gave each other a look before Zack went on to explain. "We reconnected after I retired from the military and moved back here."

"So, y'all known each other before?" Bryn guessed.

Zack nodded. "Through her ex-husband. We were friends until he fucked me over."

"Oh!" Thuy, Vida, and Bryn got the picture.

"Look at you getting with your ex's ex-best friend. You go girl!" Thuy congratulated Marsha.

"It wasn't like that." Zack defended.

He glanced at Marsha and they both lost their straight faces. "Alright maybe it was like that."

They giggled and kissed. "Good luck baby." And Marsha went on her way with Thuy and Vida.

"You so naughty." Vida teased Marsha.

"Y'all haven't lived until you got some forbidden revenge dick." Marsha blushed, and the ladies laughed.

When the crowed settled down Thuy, went on stage to make the introduction. "Hey everybody! Thanks for coming out and showing your support. It is my great pleasure to bring out our keynote speaker. She's the one that helped Vida and I during our ordeals. We don't know where we'd be without this woman. Here she is retired detective, bestselling author, and motivational speaker Marsha Brinkley."

Marsha took her place on stage and grabbed the microphone. "Hello. You heard these women's stories. They were brave enough to share their pain with the world. It's never easy. For twenty years, I've fought to help victims recover, get justice, heal and become survivors. That's what these women are, survivors. They're no longer victims. They stood up and said I'm not letting what this bastard did to me define who I am. What I am and how I think and live. Don't give your attacker the power. You have the power not them. I know they're more victims out there who remain silent. Let me say this, it's never too late to speak up. Ignoring the pain doesn't make it go away. We are now at thirty million dollars and counting. Your contributions and support will help the fight against sexual abuse and domestic violence. We can't stop and won't stop until the war is over."

The crowd applauded loudly at Marsha's speech. Then Vida went on stage to introduce Ligia. "To closeout tonight's concert we have a special treat by one of our very own board members. She is Principal of the Year, former model, and beauty queen. I present

Mrs. Ligia Sheppard!"

Ligia heard her name called and Vax gave her a kiss before she came out. "Hey y'all looking good tonight." Ligia said with charm. "This song I'm about to sang was one of my sister Sasha's favorite tunes. She lost her life at the hands of her abusive husband." She rubbed her tattoo she dedicated to Sasha's memory and flashed it to the audience. "Rest in peace, Sasha. Your baby sister misses you!"

Ligia's song of choice was *Dreamin'* by *Vanessa Williams*. She felt like she was on top of the world. Watching the crowd enjoy her beautiful voice. This moment was also bittersweet. Singing was Ligia's favorite thing to do with her sister. All she had now were the memories.

After her performance the entire audience gave a standing ovation. Ligia blew a kiss at the sky. "R.I.P. Sasha!"

"Thank you so much! You've been a wonderful audience and—" Ligia's body dropped hard on the floor and she passed out.

"Ligia!" Vax screamed in horror and ran on stage to her.

"Oh shit!" Tylisha screamed.

"Baby, baby girl!" Vax coddled Ligia in his arms. "Call an ambulance."

"Momma!" Amery cried out and tried to run to Ligia, but Enzo and Tylisha held him back.

"Amery get back." Tylisha said.

"What's wrong with, momma?" Amery continued to cry.

"Son your momma is gonna be alright." Enzo let Amery cry in his arms. "She's gonna be okay."

Jamila

Addicted to the Drama 2

Chapter 31

The paramedics burst into the Grady Hospital Emergency Room, with Ligia on a stretcher and Vax by her side. "What happened here?" The ER doctor asked.

"This is my wife! She fell out on stage!" Vax tried to remain calm, but it wasn't working.

The doctor checked Ligia's wrist for a pulse. "She has a pulse! Any medications? Medical conditions?"

"She has ovarian cancer." Tylisha answered. Obviously, she couldn't keep Ligia's secret anymore. "Dr. Moon is her doctor."

"We need to prep for examination! Stat!" The ER doctor ordered. "We might need to remove a tumor in her ovaries. We need everyone to wait out here."

"Please doctor! Please save her!" Vax begged.

"We will sir. We will."

Vax found a chair and took a seat. He cleared his mind and reality suddenly struck him. "Cancer? She has cancer!"

"She didn't want anybody to know." Tylisha explained Ligia's reasons. "She made me swear to secrecy when I found out that day you wanted me to check in on her."

"How long did she have this shit?"

Tylisha sighed. "A little after y'all came back from your honeymoon. She went into remission for a year, then it came back."

"Oh my God!" Vax covered his face.

"I've been taking her to her appointments. Making sure she takes her meds. Making sure she wasn't alone in this until she told you." Tylisha said.

"I can't lose her, I just can't!"

"You will not lose her." Enzo said. "Ligia is tough, she'll come out of this."

Vax calmed down a bit and said. "I need to call her mother."

"I already took care of that for you." Enzo volunteered. "She's on a plane right now and my parents are with her. Your kids will be here any minute." He turned to Tylisha. "I'm gonna check on Amery and see how he's doing."

Jamila

"Macal, Thuy and others are with the kids in the waiting room down the hall." Tylisha informed.

Enzo hugged and kissed Tylisha on the cheek. "Thanks for looking after Ligia."

"No problem." Tylisha looked over at Vax who was a mess. "I'll stay here with Vax, while you check on Amery."

"Alright."

Enzo went to the waiting room where everybody was. Macal went over to him and asked. "What's going on? How's Ligia?"

"They're examining her. She has ovarian cancer and she may have a tumor that needs to be removed asap." Enzo explained. "Her family is on the way. Vax is really taking this hard. Tylisha is with him. Where's Amery?"

Macal pointed. "He's over there with Thuy and Vida."

"Thanks man." Enzo walked over to Amery who was being comforted by Thuy and Vida. The ladies excused themselves so they could have a moment alone. "Hey Amery."

Amery's eyes were bright red. He was all cried out. "Dad, what's wrong with momma?"

Enzo didn't know how to answer his son's question. "Amery—"

"Please dad, tell me. I need to know!"

Enzo always taught Amery to tell it like it is and always be direct. No matter what. He needed to follow his own lessons.

He sat beside Amery and came straight out. "Your momma has cancer and she might need surgery."

"Cancer! Is momma gonna die?" Hearing the word cancer automatically made Amery fear the worst.

"That's why the doctors are with her to make sure that doesn't happen." Enzo said.

Amery dropped his head in his lap and Enzo put his arm around him. "It's gonna be okay."

Amery picked his head up and spoke. "Dad?"

"Yes son."

"Will you stay with me?"

Enzo pulled him into a hug and said. "You don't even have to ask."

Enzo couldn't bear to see Amery in pain. He'd do whatever he could to shield his son. Ligia had to pull through. He loved his best friend and it would tear his son apart if he lost his mother. For now, all Enzo could do was hold Amery's hand and hope for the best, while preparing for the worst.

****

"Xavion!" Enzo woke up from hearing someone calling out his government. He looked up and saw his older twin Bill and his beautiful wife Laura.

"Mom! Dad!" Enzo yawned and went over to his parents.

"How is she?" Laura asked with concern.

"Still no word." Enzo looked over his shoulder and saw Amery trying to wake up. "Amery, look whose here?"

Amery lit up at the sight of his grandparents. "Grandma Laura! Grandpa Bill!" He ran over to hug them.

"Amery my boy!" Bill greeted.

"Where is Emma and Nico?" Enzo asked.

"Nico is trying to help Emma pull herself together before they come inside." Laura answered.

"Hey Bill and Laura." Tylisha greeted as she entered the waiting room and Amery went into her arms for comfort.

"Tylisha darling. How are things?" Laura greeted, and Bill kissed her hand.

"Good. I'm back from getting the kids settled at my brother's." Tylisha said. "Grandma Doris is gonna drop by later today."

The doctor came in and announced. "She's awake."

"Thank God!" Enzo expressed his relief.

"You better go in one at a time." The doctor advised. "Her husband is with her now."

****

Ligia woke up in pain from the surgery. The painkillers were slowly kicking in, so it wasn't that bad. She saw Vax who had a stern look on his face.

"Hey baby! You look upset with me."

"We are husband and wife. You don't keep shit like this from me!" Vax was really pissed.

Ligia shook her head. "I didn't wanna worry you. I thought I could handle it on my own."

"Baby, I could've been there for you." Vax held her hand. "Every step of the way, I love you."

"I love you, too." Ligia kissed Vax.

A couple walked into the room. The woman looked like a slightly older version of Ligia and the man was a tall, caramel skinned man, with a black and gray beard.

"Momma, Nico!"

"Red. I'm glad you're alright." Red was Nico's pet name for Ligia.

"Thanks Nico."

"Girl don't scare us like that." Emma rushed over to her only living child and held her tight, not wanting to let her go.

"That's what I wanted to avoid." Ligia said.

"Girl if something is wrong with you tell us! You understand me?"

"I didn't wanna be a burden."

Emma shook her head. "Some things never change." She turned to Vax and shared. "When this little girl was five, she tried to cover up her colds." She turned back to Ligia. "Don't you worry about a thing. Momma's here now."

"Hey, Grandma Emma. Hey, Poppa Nico." Amery greeted as he walked in.

"Hey, baby." Emma planted a kiss on her grandson's cheek and Nico shook his hand.

"Amery, come to momma!" Ligia opened her arms wide for her son to hug her.

"Dad told me what's going on."

"He did?"

"Yes, he did."

Emma stepped out into the hall as Bill and Laura made their way in Ligia's room. She saw Enzo and Tylisha talking and walked over to them. "I hear you're the one who's been taking care of my daughter." Tylisha nodded. "Thank you so much." Emma said with deep appreciation and hugged her.

"I didn't really do anything. All I did was hold her hand. So to speak." Tylisha said.

"That's very important. It doesn't sound like much but it is." Emma gave Enzo a hug and said to Tylisha. "Make sure you take care of my other baby right here, too."

"I will, Emma." Tylisha said.

An attractive nurse with honey-toned skin and brown hair in twists, walked in the room with her clipboard. "Excuse me everyone. I need to check Mrs. Sheppard's vitals." She looked up and saw who the patient was and smiled. "Ms. Monroe?"

"Ms. Monroe? That's really a throwback right there." Ligia said.

"Don't you remember me?" The nurse asked.

Ligia took a good look at the nurse and figured out her identity. "Luvonne Benson?"

"Yeah, that's me." Luvonne confirmed. "I had you for U.S. and World History back in Southwest Fulton High."

"It's nice to see you again." Ligia hugged Luvonne. "This girl right here was one of my favorite students." She started introducing everyone who was still in the room. "This is my current husband Vax."

"How can I forget my first boss?" Luvonne hugged Vax. "Well you owned the store, but Ms. Isla hired me. We didn't see you every day. You know."

"It's good to see you again." Vax said.

"Thanks for that scholarship! I wouldn't have been able to afford nursing school without it." Luvonne said.

"You earned it!"

Ligia continued the introduction. "This is my momma and stepfather. You remember my ex-husband Xavion but we all call him Enzo and that's his fiancée Tylisha, who was taking care of me through all of this. You just missed my ex-in-laws, but they'll be back and that's my baby over there."

"Amery? I remember when you were just a little thing, when your momma would bring you to the school sometimes." Luvonne said. "You got so big and cute."

"Thanks." Amery blushed.

"How your sister Monica doing?" Ligia asked.

Luvonne checked Ligia's temperature before giving her answer. "She's doing great. Loving life at FAMU. I'll tell her you said hi."

"When you do remember to ask about Mrs. Goss." Ligia said.

"Alrighty." Luvonne wrote down the numbers on the machine on the clipboard. "It was great seeing you again."

"You too."

When Luvonne left Tylisha was slightly confused. "Mrs. Goss?"

Ligia let out a giggle. "Luvonne was with me when I first started teaching. Around the end of her sophomore year I found out I was pregnant and married Enzo. When she had me again her senior year it was hard for her and the rest of the class to call me Mrs. Goss. Let alone Mrs. Sheppard if they see me now as you just witnessed."

"That's not the case with Monica." Ligia added. "My last name was Goss for ten years. If former students call me by my maiden name that makes me feel really old. If they call me Mrs. Sheppard that means they're babies." She joked.

"I'm back." Luvonne said. "I forgot to check your blood pressure Ms. Monroe."

"That's okay, baby." Ligia sat up and let Luvonne check her blood pressure. "How are things going for you?"

"I love being a nurse. I'm happily married, to a pediatrician and we have three boys and a girl." Luvonne said.

"I'm so happy to see you doing well." Ligia said.

"And thank you for everything. You mean more to me than you'll ever know." Luvonne managed to hold back the tears and hugged Ligia."

"Anytime baby! Anytime!"

Chapter 32

Fallon was hard at work in the activity room, painting a still life portrait of the garden outside from memory.

"It's beautiful." Rita complimented.

"Thanks Rita." Fallon said.

It took a while, but Rita got comfortable enough to open up to Fallon. Rita's mother cheated on Rita's father and left him for her side nigga. Rita's stepfather was a well-respected businessman on the outside, but on the inside, he was a cruel, evil, bastard who abused and raped Rita, while her mother sat back and did nothing.

Rita was threatened to keep quiet about the abuse. It didn't take long for Rita to learn that money and power was more important to her selfish, greedy, bitch mother than her daughter's well-being.

Rita found out she was pregnant, with her stepfather's baby, and tried to take her own life. She miscarried as a result of her suicide attempt. Her stepfather was arrested and her mother publicly disowned Rita and went as far as testifying against her during the trial. Rita's tragic story ended with her being sent to Wadley.

"You seem very happy today." Fallon said.

"Daddy's coming to visit me today."

"That's great."

"How's your Aunt Naomi?" Rita asked.

"She's great." Fallon answered. "She and her boyfriend are visiting me tomorrow."

"Who was that lady and her kids who visited you last week?" Rita asked.

"My former sister-in-law." Fallon answered.

"She seems very nice."

"Yes, she is. So, is her grandmother. She makes the best cakes and macaroni and cheese." Fallon boasted. "Where does your father live?"

"He lives in Savannah now. If I ever get out of here, he said I could live with him." Rita sounded very doubtful.

"You will someday." Fallon encouraged. "Trust me. I gotta remind myself all the time to take it one day at a time."

Jamila

Fallon went back to her painting. Rita sat, watching Fallon work and admired her talent. "Will you teach me how to paint?"

"Of course." Fallon agreed.

"Rita!" A man's voice called out.

Rita looked up to see who called her and smiled. "Daddy!"

"Sugarplum!" Her father greeted his little girl with a big hug. "How are you?"

"I'm making it."

"You're in great spirits." Rita's father commented.

"I have a roommate who is very nice to me. She's beautiful, smart, and a great artist. She's sort of like the momma I always wanted."

Rita's sweet kind words touched Fallon's heart.

"You wanna meet her? She's over here." Rita pointed in Fallon's direction.

"If you insist." Rita's father went with the flow.

"Fallon, this is my daddy." Fallon stopped her painting to meet Rita's father.

This man was fine. Skin like expresso, shinning white teeth, well-built body, neatly trimmed goatee, and Larry Fitzgerald type dreadlocks.

"His name is, Chester. Daddy, this is the nice lady I told you about."

"It's a pleasure to meet you." Fallon greeted and shook his hand. *What strong hands!*

"Same here." Chester's strong sexy voice greeted back. "I appreciate you for showing my daughter kindness. She really needs it."

"Rita is a special girl." Fallon said.

"Yes, my baby girl is." Chester wrapped Rita in his arms and kissed her forehead. "I'll let you get back to your painting. Very beautiful."

"Thanks." Fallon said. "I worked very hard on it."

I was talking about the painter! Chester thought.

152

Chapter 33

"Happy birthday, baby!" Tylisha kissed Enzo at his birthday party at Golden City.

They were cuddled up at the booth, where his birthday presents were gathered.

"Thanks baby." Enzo said.

"You got a lot of gifts."

"Yeah, I just feel the love." Enzo flashed a big sexy smile.

"I'd give you my present, but considering what it is, you gotta wait until we get home." Tylisha winked.

"Uh huh." Enzo rubbed Tylisha's ass at the hint.

"Sorry we're late." Vax said with Ligia in tow.

"Here's our present." Ligia placed their gift on the table.

"Thanks." Enzo hugged Vax. "Glad y'all came." He then hugged Ligia and expressed his concern. "Do you think it's wise for you to be out and about this soon?"

Ligia appreciated everyone's concern for her these past two weeks. It was annoying but sweet. "Enzo I'm fine. Like Tylisha said. I got cancer. That bitch don't got me."

"Exactly." Tylisha declared and hugged Ligia.

"Come on baby, let's dance." Ligia pulled Vax to the dance-floor.

****

"Looks like Enzo is having a good time." Thuy said as she, Vida and Bryn were enjoying their drinks.

"Yes, he is." Vida said. "Thuy you sure you don't miss me?"

"I's been almost a month since you moved in with Sam. I think I've gotten used to the peace and quiet and fucking Macal all over my house." Thuy laughed.

Bryn saw Ligia dancing with Vax in all smiles. Really enjoying life. "That Ligia, is a real trooper."

"Yes, she is." Thuy agreed.

"How are things with you and Macal?" Bryn asked.

"They're going great." Thuy said. "He's taking me on a vacation to Tahiti this weekend."

"What's going on with that business deal y'all doing together?" Vida asked.

"It's still going. It may be a shitload of work but it's very rewarding."

Thuy saw Macal and Enzo whispering to each other before coming her way. "Here he is." Thuy got out of her seat to be in her man's arms.

"What's up, everybody?" Macal greeted. "Having a good time?"

"Yes, we are." Vida exclaimed.

"What were you and Enzo whispering about?" Thuy asked.

"Wait for it?" Macal glanced over at Enzo and Tylisha at their booth.

"Wait for what?" Bryan asked.

"Look over at Enzo and Tylisha." The trio turned their heads to look and Macal snapped. "Don't look!"

Thuy gave Macal a crazy look and smacked his arm. "Nigga don't do that! I hate it when people do that shit."

"Telling somebody to look and they don't really mean it!" Vida scolded.

"Makeup your fucking mind." Bryn added on.

"Like I'm the only one who ever done it before?" Macal defended and everyone laughed.

****

"You are looking beautiful tonight." Enzo said to Tylisha, checking out her body in her sexy green dress.

"Thanks." Tylisha blushed. "You the one who bought this dress and wanted me to wear it tonight for some reason."

"You're right, there is a reason." Enzo patted his lap. "Sit right there, Tylisha."

"Ooh, the best seat in the house." Tylisha teased and took her seat, positioning herself, so her ass could get a good feel of Enzo's dick print.

"This is one of the best birthdays of my life. I have everything a man could ask for except one thing." Enzo gently rubbed her cheek. "Hopefully you can change that for me."

"Me—how?"

Enzo held Tylisha's hand and expressed himself. "Baby girl, you mean the world to me. Every day with you, is like Heaven on Earth. The way you make me feel. The way you stimulate my mind, body, and soul. The way you love my son, like you do your own children, who I also carry with me like my own. The way you supported my best friend shows me how pure and golden your heart is. I am so lucky to have you in my life." He took a deep breath, before making his main point. "What I'm trying to say is, I love you and I want you to be my wife."

Tylisha jumped off Enzo's lap shocked. "Enzo are you serious, you wanna marry me?"

"Yes, I do." Enzo pulled out a jewelry box and got on bended knee. He opened the box revealing a twenty-four-carat diamond ring. "Tylisha, will you marry me?"

Tylisha was filled with joy. "Yes, Enzo, I will marry you!"

Enzo placed the ring on her finger. He turned to Macal and the others and announced. "She said yes y'all!"

Everyone bum rushed in their direction. "Congratulations!" They all cheered for the newly engaged couple.

"Thank you so much!" Tylisha flashed the rock and the ladies were in awe.

"Yeah, I gave him permission to ask your hand in marriage." Macal said to Tylisha.

"Boy you need to stop your shit." Tylisha laughed at Macal.

"My baby sister is getting married!" Macal pulled Tylisha into a hug and kissed her forehead.

"Thanks, Macal." Tylisha said.

"Enzo, you better be good to her." Macal said.

"Don't worry man, I will." Enzo gave Macal dap.

"I'm about to get us a round of champagne." Macal volunteered.

"Thanks." Tylisha said.

Jamila

Macal went over to the bar and got the bartender's attention. "What can I get for you sir?"

"I'd like a round of champagne for the Goss birthday party."

"Coming right up." The bartender said.

While Macal was waiting for the bartender to come back, a woman with a succulent body, and a grotesque face greeted Macal flirtatiously. "Hey!"

Macal managed to hold in his disgust and greeted back, without being rude. "Hey."

Macal tried to ease his way to the other end of the bar, but the woman stopped him. "What's the hurry?"

"I'm waiting on this order, so I can get back to my woman and friend's party."

The bartender came back. "I got your champagne ready."

Thank God. "Thanks." Macal pulled out his wallet to pay for the champagne and tipped the bartender.

The multiple fifty and hundred-dollar bills and credit cards in Macal's wallet, made the woman's pussy drip. She had to snatch him up.

Fuck his woman. "Is your dick as thick as your wallet?"

"Hey baby, what's the hold up?" Thuy appeared out of nowhere and Macal was relieved.

"Just paying for the champagne." Macal said.

The ugly woman looked at Thuy with scorn. "This bitch is your woman?"

Being called a bitch in that manner automatically put Thuy, in Stomp-A-Hoe mode. She knew exactly who this hoe was. "It's your ass!"

"You know this woman." Macal asked Thuy using the term woman loosely to describe the fucked up faced thot.

"This is one of the many hoes Jeromy cheated on me with." Macal was in disbelief. Some niggas will stick their dick in anything. At least he fucked bitches who actually look good. "Are you serious?"

Thuy nodded. "He brought this hoe back to the house to fuck, but I beat their trifling nasty asses home, waiting on them with

156

Bryn's belt!"

"That shit was funny as hell." Bryn giggled to Tylisha.

"Your ass was lucky." The ugly thot dismissed. "That was some fuck shit you did! Throwing my man in prison and lying on him all over T.V."

"You dumb, ugly, ass bitch!" Thuy yelled. "That nigga tried to kill me!"

"He told me he didn't do it!" The ugly woman yelled. "He loves me and when he gets out he's gonna marry me. Who do you think keeps money on his books and makes sure he's straight?"

Like I give a shit! Thuy glanced over at the crew, they all shared a snicker. They found the bitch's stupidity quite amusing.

Even Lolette ain't this crazy and stupid! Tylisha thought.

"Your ass is dumber than I thought." Thuy laughed and mocked. It was very laughable that this hoe was pathetic enough to eat the bullshit Jeromy was feeding her.

"No! You the dumb bitch, for trying to pin a baby on my man, and stab him in the fucking back after he tried to save your ungrate-ful ass!" The hoe hurled out her nonsense.

Thuy turned to the newly engaged couple. "Tylisha—Enzo. Hopefully, one day you'll understand why I had to do what I had to do on y'all special night." Thuy rolled up on the ugly bitch and gave her a stinging backhand to the face. The impact of the slap made the hoe hit her head on the bar. "Bitch don't you ever motherfucking come for me again!" Thuy warned as she pointed in the bitch's ugly ass face.

Macal pulled Thuy close to him and asked. "Are you okay, baby?"

"I'm good. Let's get back to the party." They walked past the ugly thot still holding her face where she was slapped. "Next time bitch stay in your place, in the hoe-lane or get ran the fuck over!"

The party went on like nothing happened. Tylisha whispered to Macal on the sly. "Looks like you got a rough neck."

"Yeah" Macal agreed. "Wait a minute. You're not gonna accuse me of trying to fuck that bitch?"

Tylisha shook her head. "I know you. Even you're not stupid

enough to try to get new pussy in your woman's presence. You maybe a hoe, but you a hoe with standards."

"Right." Macal found Thuy to check on her. "You okay, baby?"

"I'm good." Thuy nodded.

Macal still couldn't believe how ugly that bitch was, and that any nigga would let her anywhere near their dick. "Jeromy cheated on you with that?"

"Yes, the nigga did."

"Damn. That bitch looked like she got hit in the face, with a bag of nickels!" Macal joked and everyone laughed.

"Not even Jett and his former fellow inmates was ever that desperate for pussy!" Thuy giggled. "I had to show that bastard and bitch what time it was after I left Lullaby Deluxe."

"Lullaby Deluxe?" Tylisha asked.

"That's the store where I ran into that nice Fallon woman." Thuy said. "In fact, it was that very night."

"That's right it was." Vida said. "After you met her, we had to beat Jeromy and the hoe home, because you overheard them on the phone when this nigga butt dialed you by accident."

"The weird thing is that she has the same name as Macal's first wife." Thuy said to her friends. "Talk about a crazy coincidence."

Not! Tylisha screamed internally.

Chapter 34

Tomorrow was the start of Ligia's chemotherapy treatments. Vax, Amery, and the rest of her friends and family had been showing their love and support. Vax, Ligia and Amery were all in the bedroom by Ligia's side, until the doorbell rung and Vax went to answer the door.

"Dave, what are you doing here?" Clearly Vax wasn't expecting the family attorney to stop by.

"Ligia, called me." Dave said.

"Dave, you made it." Ligia appeared at the door. "You can wait for us in the dining room."

Dave went into the living room and Vax whispered to Ligia. "What's our attorney doing here?"

"You'll find out when Enzo and Tylisha get here." Ligia whispered back. "They're on the way."

This wife of mine sure can surprise a nigga! "Baby what's going on?"

"You know my chemo starts tomorrow. I need to make important arrangements just in case." She uncomfortably explained.

"Please don't talk like that. You're gonna beat this."

"Hopefully, but still we need to be prepared." The doorbell rang, Ligia knew who it was. "There they are. Let them in while I talk to Amery."

"Alright." Vax said, then answered the door. "Hello, come on in." He let Enzo, Tylisha and the kids into the house.

"I brought the kids, because they wanted to cheer Amery up." Tylisha said.

"I think he'll like that." Vax said. "There he is now."

"Hey, everyone." Amery greeted his father, future stepmother, and step siblings.

"How are you son?" Enzo asked.

"Doing okay. Trying to look after momma."

"And momma really appreciates you, baby." Ligia held Amery in her arms tight and kissed his cheek. "Why don't you take Welton and Ayla to the studio while we handle some business?"

"Okay." Amery said.

"Aunt Ligia, I made this for you." Ayla handed Ligia a drawing. It was a get well soon drawing of a teddy bear, dressed as a doctor, giving a hug to a cute drawing version of Ligia in a pink hospital gown in the bed smiling.

"Awe! That's so sweet, baby." Ligia kissed Ayla. "Thanks sweetheart."

When the kids went on their way, Enzo asked Ligia. "What's up? You said this was important."

"It is, follow me." Everyone followed Ligia into the dining room, where Dave was waiting, they took their seats.

"This is Dave Hogan our attorney. Dave this is my ex-husband and Amery's father Xavion, and his fiancée Tylisha." Ligia introduced.

"Pleasure to meet you." Enzo shook Dave's hand.

"You're preparing a will, aren't you?' Tylisha guessed.

"Yes." Ligia confirmed. "Let's face it. You need to be prepared. You don't know what can happen tomorrow. Do y'all have a will?" She asked Enzo and Tylisha.

"I don't." Tylisha answered.

"Me neither." Enzo shook his head. "My parents drew theirs up ten years ago."

"Ligia is right." Dave said. "It's never too early to draw up a will. You never know what can happen."

"Exactly." Vax understood Ligia's reasons.

"You're keeping your will the same right?" Dave asked Vax.

"That's correct. The last time I updated my will, it was when my daughter had her last baby." Vax said.

"Alright good." Dave said. "Are you ready to get started?"

"Yes." Ligia said.

Dave skimmed through the documents, then got down to business. "First the custody of your son Amery will go to his father until he's of age?"

"That's correct." Ligia said.

"Your wedding rings from your marriage to Xavion will go to your son as well?"

"Right." Ligia figured she'd give the rings to Amery, if he ever found the right girl to marry, he could use them to propose to her.

"Your clothes and jewelry will be donated to the Restart Project Foundation."

"Yes."

"Speaking of which there's the matter of your seat on the board of the foundation. Who will you leave it to?" Dave asked.

"Tylisha." Ligia answered.

Tylisha was caught completely off guard. "Are you sure?"

"Yes, I'm sure." Ligia said. "You'll be perfect. Will you take my place if the unknown happens?"

Tylisha was still unsure about this but went along with it anyway. "Alright, I'll do it."

"Thanks."

Dave continued. "Moving on to your assets. There's your portion of the Sheppard estate, your divorce settlement from your previous marriage and etc."

"That'll be equally divided by my mother, stepfather and son." Ligia said.

"Amelia Dixon, Nicolas Dixon and Amery Goss." Dave listed the heirs respectively.

"That's correct."

"You do realize until your son is of age his portion of your estate will be in the control of his legal guardian which would be Xavion?" Dave pointed out.

"What do y'all think?" Ligia asked everyone. "I don't want there to be any problems or hard feelings."

"There won't be. Everybody here is mature with good sense." Tylisha said and Enzo nodded in agreement.

"We're all here for you and want what's best for you and Amery." Vax said, kissing Ligia's hand.

"Thanks." Ligia turned her attention back to Dave. "Go ahead and proceed with the original plan."

"Alright." Dave said. "Your son will also have your possessions and mementos?"

"Right." Ligia said. "Vax, will have my wedding ring from our marriage, my portion of the properties, and everything that was accumulated during our marriage."

"It looks like everything has been addressed. I'll draw this up and send you a copy to sign." Dave gathered the documents.

"Thank you so much." Ligia shook Dave's hand.

"Anytime, good day to you all." Dave said.

"I'll see you to the door." Vax said.

"Are you ready?" Tylisha asked Ligia.

Ligia sighed. "I'm as ready as I'm gonna be."

"Are you sure?"

"It's gonna happen eventually."

"Alright."

Ligia and Tylisha went straight to the bedroom. Ligia sat in front of her vanity mirror and Tylisha got the scissors ready and pulled a zip lock bag out of her purse. "Go ahead." Ligia said.

Ligia closed her eyes as Tylisha started to cut off her long, naturally, curly uniquely brown and red blended locks. Tylisha cut the hair and put it in the zip lock bag to donate to Locks of Love as Ligia requested.

"All finished." Tylisha said.

Ligia opened her eyes and looked in the mirror. Her hair was now shorter than a fingernail. She was speechless.

"It's just hair. Look at it this way. You'll save more money and time. Now all you gotta do is throw on a nice wig. Girl your lace fronts are gonna be off the chain!" Tylisha tried to help Ligia look on the bright side.

"But wigs gotta come off sooner or later." Ligia spoke weakly trying not to cry. "What about Vax? What's he goinna think now that I'm baldheaded? Is he still gonna think I'm beautiful and desirable? Is he even gonna wanna touch me, let alone make love to me?"

Ligia felt someone lift her out of her chair and plant a fat kiss on her. "Did that answer your silly question?" Vax asked.

"I think it did." Ligia let out a chuckle.

"Baby girl, you are a beautiful woman, nothing in this world is gonna make me think otherwise."

"Awe Vax." Ligia kissed Vax. They were so into making out

they forgot Tylisha was still in the room."

"I'll leave you crazy kids alone." Tylisha said.

While still kissing Ligia Vax waved at Tylisha like he was saying goodbye and beat it.

Tylisha exited the room, closing the door behind her.

"How is she?" Enzo asked.

Ligia let out a loud pleasurable moan.

"I think she'll be fine." Tylisha assumed.

Ligia moaned again.

"Right." Enzo agreed. "Let's go."

Tylisha knocked on the door. "Alright we're gonna take off."

"Alright and take Amery with you." Ligia said in between moans.

"Cool." Enzo said. "I'll bring him back tomorrow after your treatment."

"Great!" Ligia's moaning grew louder.

"We better get out of here, she's about to nut." Enzo whispered, then he and Tylisha made their way downstairs.

"How do you know?" Tylisha asked.

Enzo stopped in his tracks and gave Tylisha a crazy look. "She used to be my wife and had my only child."

"Oh."

"Yeah."

"I'm getting jealous." Tylisha pouted. "Unlike them when we get home we gotta settle with quiet sex." The price for having a house full of kids.

"When did you start having quiet sex?" Enzo sarcastically asked. Knowing damn well Tylisha woke up the dead the way he put it on her.

"Oh, what the fuck ever."

"Uh huh." Enzo swatted Tylisha's ass. "Let's go home and try to have quiet sex."

"Quiet, loud, don't matter as long as I get that dick."

Jamila

Chapter 35

"Here we are, front and center!" Macal cheered, showing Thuy the Business Weekly article on his phone, with their picture in the headline. They were having dinner at a restaurant in Downtown Atlanta celebrating the launch of their business venture.

"Yes, we are." Thuy shared Macal's excitement. "Green Safe Services is now open for business."

"Thanks to your clientele we had a terrific head start." Macal said.

"It felt great sitting in your chair at your desk."

"The king shares the throne with his queen."

"Thanks, my king." Thuy blushed and let Macal kiss her hand. "Isn't Enzo and Tylisha supposed to be joining us?"

"Yeah, they had to stop by Vax and Ligia's house first to drop the kids off and check on Ligia." Macal said.

"Ligia is really not letting cancer control her life. She's going through her treatments, still working and keeping up her daily routines." Thuy said in admiration. "She was in excellent spirits at the board meeting yesterday."

"With Tylisha as your unofficial life coach, you'd think you can move mountains." Macal slightly exaggerated. "Grandma Doris, has been helping Ligia out as well."

A waiter came up to their table with a cake and placed it in front of Thuy. "Desert for the beautiful lady."

"I didn't order anything yet." Thuy corrected.

"It's on the house." The waiter said.

"Thuy, maybe you should take it." Macal suggested. "Who knows? The cake might be good."

"Alright Ike." Thuy joked.

Macal grabbed Thuy and kissed her hard on the cheek. "That's my Anna Mae." He joked back.

The waiter chuckled under his breath, getting the banter, and walked off.

Thuy grabbed the fork and picked through the cake. "Chocolate fudge cake with whipped cream and—" She noticed something shining in the whipped cream. She used her fork for further exami-nation. "Is that a ring?" Thuy pulled the ring out of the whipped cream and wiped it off. It was a perfectly cut sparkling diamond made with the finest platinum. "Shit it's huge and beautiful!"

"Yes, it is. Just like my future wife."

"Your future wife?" Thuy glanced at Macal.

"That would be the sexy cutie pie holding the ring." Macal hinted.

Thuy was speechless. "What the fuck?"

"First let me clean this off." Macal took the ring back. He dipped some paper towels in a water glass and wiped the ring off clean.

"You are one crazy negro." Thuy laughed. "First Enzo, now you." She had a pretty good idea what was about to happen next.

"Thuy you are my beautiful queen. I love you, baby girl and I want to spend the rest of my life with you." Macal grabbed her hand and prepared to drop the big question. "Will you give this crazy ne-gro the honor and privilege of being his wife? Thuy Mackenzie El-lis, will you marry me?"

"Alright, I guess I'll marry you Macal Jordy Kilborn." Thuy gave her big answer in a playful nonchalant manner.

"You, silly girl." Macal giggled, sliding the beautiful rock on Thuy's finger.

"We're about to be husband and wife. We can be silly together." Thuy giggled, kissing Macal.

"The fuck you are!" Macal and Thuy looked up and there stood a highly pissed off Lolette.

"This bitch!" Thuy snapped.

"Lolette what the fuck are you doing here?" Macal was not hav-ing Lolette's bullshit today.

Lolette pointed at Thuy. "You marrying this bitch? After eve-rything we've shared and been though together?"

Macal got out of his seat and stood face to face with Lolette with authority. "Look, we didn't share shit. It was just a fuck. Now get the fuck over it. Can't you see that I'm with my fiancée?"

Lolette looked Macal up and down. "Oh, now you wanna act all

Addicted to the Drama 2

brand new because of this stick up million-dollar hoe?"

"Bitch what the fuck did I tell you about talking about my woman like that?" Macal hissed in Lolette's face.

Look at my future hubby defending my honor. So sexy. Thuy blushed. Watching Macal going in on that bitch to protect her, made Thuy fall deeper in love with him. No man had ever stood up for her and protected her like this before. This masculine protection was making Thuy cream in her thong.

"Nigga, fuck that bitch!" Lolette looked over at Thuy, "And I see your ass ain't got shit to say. I still owe your ass for trying to swing on me!"

Thuy let out a little scoff and replied calmly. "Darling, I didn't try to swing on you. I laid that ass out. Obviously, you forgot about our little talk and the result of your lack of cooperation."

"Lolette get the fuck out of here, now." Macal ordered.

Lolette smiled. "I'll go." She was about to leave, but not before dropping a bomb. "By the way Macal. Thanks for the fuck in the limo. Too bad Fallon ruined it by trying to kill us in that accident." She then said to Thuy. "Oh, don't mind us reminiscing about our past fucks. You were too busy getting faked carjacked and shot up while Macal was making me nut. Good day and happy engagement." On that note Lolette made her exit in triumph.

This was not the way Thuy was supposed to find out about the accident.

Macal was so embarrassed. "Baby I am so sorry. Let me explain." But Thuy wasn't in her seat.

All that was left of her was a pair of silver earrings and a pair of gray Louboutin Red Bottom pumps. In all his years on this earth, Macal, knew no matter in public or in private, or social status or background. He knew the universal meaning of a black woman taking off her earrings and shoes.

"Oh shit." Macal sprinted out of the restaurant to try to stop the unthinkable.

****

Jamila

Lolette strutted to her car like she was the shit. She didn't have a care in the world. The way she busted up Macal's marriage proposal to the bitch was epic. She was about to open her car door but was stopped by a hard tug on her hair.

Thuy spun Lolette around. *Whap!* Thuy, slapped her hard across the face and jacked her up by her collar.

"What the fuck did I tell you?" Thuy yelled in Lolette's face.

Lolette tried say something. "Uh—"

"What did I say?"

"But—"

"What did I say?" Thuy held onto Lolette's collar tight, slightly dragging her around like she was a ragdoll.

"You said that—that—that—that—"

"I said that—that—that—that—what?" Thuy viciously mocked. "Let me refresh your memory you dumb ass bitch!" She didn't even wait for a response. "You better stay the fuck away from my man. If I catch your nasty, scandalous, ass anywhere near my man again. If I even have an ounce of an inkling that you've been anywhere near Macal, I'm gonna finish Fallon's motherfucking job! You understand me?" Thuy smiled, letting Lolette go.

Thuy marched away from the scene in a huff not noticing she was passing Tylisha and Enzo who saw the whole thing.

Tylisha didn't miss the opportunity to laugh at Lolette, which pissed her off further.

"This shit ain't funny!" She yelled in shame.

"Yes, it is. I think you met your match. You might not wanna fuck with her." Tylisha warned snickering.

Lolette refused to be defeated. "I ain't done with—."

"You want your eyes to match?" Tylisha dished out a threat of her own in a more intimidating tone.

"No." Lolette answered.

"Then close your forever dick, sucking, mouth and kick rocks." Tylisha sent Lolette on her way.

She and Enzo found Macal and Thuy in the parking lot.

"Baby I wanted to tell you." Macal said to Thuy, but she wasn't having it.

168

"Is there anything else you wanna tell me about that hoe?" She asked, snatching her shoes and earrings out of Macal's hands, so she could put them back on.

"Uh—"

"Uh—nothing." Thuy interrupted. "We're gonna settle this shit right motherfucking now. You better tell me everything." Thuy pulled out her phone and pulled up Google. "You better tell me before Google does."

"I cheated on Fallon with Lolette, we were all in the limo, that almost ran you and Jeromy off the road." Macal blurted out. "She's the same Fallon you met at Lullaby Deluxe."

"Is that why y'all are divorced?" Thuy assumed. "Because she snapped and tried to kill your lying, cheating, ass and that ratchet ass hoe?"

"That's in the past." Macal insisted. "I'm a changed man."

Bullshit. Tylisha and Enzo shared the same thought.

"Don't let Lolette mess up what we're building." Macal said.

Thuy wasn't sure about anything. This man had some serious baggage. Not to mention, she shared some strange connection with this man's first wife. How could she go through with the wedding with this new information? She needed time to think.

"Macal I don't know if I can handle this. I love you and want to marry you, but you can't be having—"

"Baby, I love you." Macal pulled Thuy in his strong arms not letting her get away. "Don't worry about bitter ass Lolette. You are the woman I wanna marry. You know, I love you. Don't I prove it every day?" He planted a kiss on her lips. "And every night?" He kissed her again.

"Ummm." Thuy's protective wall was slowly crumbling and they kissed again.

"Let's take care of our business with Tylisha and Enzo. Afterwards, I'll take you home and make it up to you all night along."

"Okay, baby." Thuy giggled and the two went back into the restaurant.

Enzo and Tylisha couldn't believe what they'd just witnessed, as they watched Macal and Thuy walk in the restaurant like a newly engaged couple in love. Like they didn't have a confrontation dealing with a side bitch less than a moment ago.

"How the fuck does he do it?" Enzo was highly impressed at Macal's ability to get out of impossible, shitty situations very smoothly.

"I don't know." Tylisha took note of Enzo's tone of awe at her philandering brother. "Your ass better not be taking notes. I know that much."

Enzo put his hands up in defense. "Whoa baby, you're mad at your brother. Not your future husband."

"You just keep acting right or I shall have to fuck you up." Tylisha knew Enzo wasn't stupid enough to cheat on her, but a few heeding reminders never hurt.

"Yes dear." Enzo played along and kissed Tylisha on her cheek, before joining Macal and Thuy in the restaurant.

    ****

"Ah, shit, make me cum nigga!" Lolette screamed, letting Macal beat her pussy up, with her legs in the air, while flat on her back on her living room floor.

"This pussy is good, girl!" Macal moaned, savoring the tightness and wetness of the pussy.

"Ah!" Lolette came hard, then let Macal have his complete way with her. Making her cum and moan.

"That's it, baby." Macal grunted, pounding the pussy harder. "Nut on this dick, yeah, ah!"

Macal felt himself about to nut and pulled out of Lolette. He climbed off of her and got on his feet. "Suck on my shit, bitch!" He ordered.

Lolette got on her knees and jammed the dick in her mouth. She sucked hard on the pole that was covered with her juices. She sucked on that dick like she was trying to take the skin off. Lolette knew, no matter what she did Macal, couldn't get enough of her sex. Macal shot his seed in her mouth hitting her tonsils. She held her head back and gulped his seed down. Still winded, Macal and

Lolette laid on top of each other on the floor.

Lolette kissed his lips. "Macal, I love you." She spoke softly.

"You do, huh?" Macal stroked her hair. He put on the charm without actually saying the 'L' word back. How could he love a woman like Lolette? She was a disloyal bitch, but a sexy disloyal bitch, with some mean ass pussy. He knew he needed to break this habit. He'd tried so hard, but not hard enough.

"Yes baby, I do love you." Lolette said. "I never felt this way about any man before."

Macal replied in a sweet sexy tone. "I know you love me, baby, but you can't be acting all crazy like that and getting in Thuy's face."

"I can't help it." She whined. "She stole you from me."

"I was never yours to begin with." Macal rubbed her cheek.

"I wish you could give me a chance. I fought so hard for us and put up with so much."

Macal kissed Lolette. "I understand baby, but you gotta promise me something."

"Yes baby?"

"Promise me that you'll behave and be good." Lolette nodded.

Macal got off the floor to get dressed. "You're not gonna get in Thuy's face, either right?"

"Right." Lolette said. "Since we're making promises can you make me one?"

"Anything baby."

"Promise me you won't marry, Thuy, and you'll give our love a chance." Lolette requested.

Macal, kissed her with deep lustful passion. "I promise baby."

Macal, got on his feet and got dressed.

"When will I see you again?" Lolette asked.

"I'll drop by tomorrow at around four o'clock."

Lolette flashed a seductive smile and spread her legs wide. She rubbed her cum covered clit and said. "Me and my pussy will be counting the minutes."

Jamila

Chapter 36

Tylisha had to drop by Macal's penthouse real quick, because she left the floor plans, and her portfolio of the samples she was going to use to decorate Macal's new mansion which was now completely built. She used her key to the penthouse to let herself inside since she knew he wasn't home.

Tylisha went straight to the office and found what she was looking for on the table. "Here they are." She grabbed the items. "Now I'm outta here."

Tylisha went downstairs and headed for the door. She opened the door and was met with foolishness.

"Macal!" Lolette screamed out at the top of her lungs. She pushed Tylisha out of her way letting herself in the penthouse.

Tylisha felt like she'd just had an outer body experience. *Did this bitch just push me out the way and barge in my brother's house like that?*

"Macal! Macal! Macal!" Lolette was heard yelling all over the house like a madwoman, as she searched far and wide for the nigga who stood her up again.

"Macal, Macal, nigga where the fuck you at?" Lolette continued to scream like a damn fool throughout her search. She entered the office and looked around. "Macal, Mac—"

Lolette was stopped by Tylisha lifting Lolette off her feet just a tad and throwing her on the couch. "Now I let you slide, pushing me out the way, barging into my brother's place of residence. But, if you don't calm the fuck down and start acting like you got some damn sense, you're gonna be picking your teeth off the motherfucking floor!"

Lolette was about to retort, when Tylisha had to shut that ass down. "Keep in mind that unlike the hospital, this time ain't nobody around to break this up. Now what the fuck is your problem?"

"That nigga stood me up." Lolette was filled with rage. "His ass was supposed to come by my house at four o'clock, he never showed up. I checked his office, he ain't there. Where the fuck can he be?"

"He just left." Tylisha volunteered.

Lolette was taken aback by the unpleasant surprise. "What the fuck you mean he just left?" She yelled with fire in her lungs.

"Watch your tone." Tylisha replied calmly with a smile. "Now ask that question again, but this time like someone with some home training and maybe you might get an answer."

Lolette was annoyed as fuck. She took a breather to calm down. She was desperate, but in order to get to the bottom of Macal's latest fuckery stunt she had to play nice in the sandbox with Little Miss Wannabe Queen Bee. No matter how demeaning the shit was.

"Tylisha, if it's not too much trouble would you tell me where Macal is? I would really appreciate it." Lolette politely requested. She knew that, in order to increase her chances, she had to top it off with the magic word. "Please."

"See that wasn't so hard." Tylisha said with delight. "Since I'm in a good mood and this is the first time in history you acted like a good behaving human being. I'll go ahead and answer your question. Macal and Thuy eloped."

Did I hear her correctly! "They eloped?"

"Yes, they took off after we all bid them farewell this morning." Tylisha informed.

That motherfucker played me for that bitch! Lolette was seething. "He told me he wasn't gonna marry her and that he'd give us a chance. He told me that shit last night!" Her face turned bright red, she started bawling like a baby. "How the fuck could he do this to me? I love him so much!"

Tylisha handed Lolette a box of Kleenex to wipe her tears and took a seat next to her. "Lolette, you knew how Macal operated. That man fucked around on his first wife with you, who was supposed to be her best friend and along with who knows how many other women. Now he's doing the same shit to Thuy."

Lolette wiped her tears, sniffled a bit and quietly listened to Tylisha. "The reason he comes to you is not because he loves you. He doesn't love you. He loves your availability. He knows no matter what he can still get the pussy. It's the same with all his other side pieces. When y'all get out of line, he'll say and do whatever he gotta do to pacify y'all enough to not fuck up his good thing with his main chick."

"You are a beautiful woman, Lolette. You can have any single man you want." Tylisha stressed the word single. "Woman to woman. You need to change your ways and fix your inner conflicts, I know you have them. If you don't you'll never be happy. You'll end up alone or worse. Let Macal go and get your life right. Before it's too late."

Tylisha got off the couch and offered Lolette her hand. "Let's go."

Lolette took Tylisha's hand, she helped her off the couch. The ladies walked downstairs, into the parking lot.

Before, Lolette got in her car she said. "Tylisha, I know you hate me but, thanks."

"You welcome." Tylisha rubbed Lolette's back, "Just think about what I said."

"Okay." Lolette said, but deep down Tylisha knew better. That hoe will never change. She'll be back stronger and more ratchet than ever.

Jamila

Chapter 37

"Here we are. Las Vegas, Sin City!" Macal exclaimed all snuggled up with Thuy in the backseat of a golden Rolls Royce, being chauffeured around. Compliments of one of their Green Safe clients who'd won the Mega Millions jackpot.

Thuy smiled and kissed Macal. "Eloping to Las Vegas. Oh, how original darling." She said with sarcasm.

"Oh baby. Your sarcasm makes my dick hard." Macal rubbed her ass.

"I know." Thuy giggled and switched to serious mode. "By the way. No pussy until we're husband wife."

"Since you put it that way. Let's hurry up and do this."

"Nasty ass freak." Thuy giggled.

"Yeah, you love that nasty ass shit." Macal slapped Thuy's ass hard.

"Yeah, I do." She confessed with glow.

They arrived at the Mandalay Bay Resort and Casino where they were gonna have their wedding on the beach and spend the first part of their honeymoon. The staff welcomed them and gave them a tour of the hotel. The accommodations were luxurious. The wedding set up on the beach was beautiful. They saw the casino and their honeymoon suite they'd be staying in after they got married.

After the tour Macal and Thuy, had to go their separate ways to get ready for the wedding. "Well this is it." Macal said.

"Our last moments being single." Thuy said.

"One last kiss before we become Mr. and Mrs. Kilborn?" Macal requested.

"Okay." Thuy giggled and let Macal kiss her. "See you soon."

"You too." Macal said.

The two went their separate ways to prepare to become man and wife unaware that someone was lurking nearby watching their every move.

****

Jamila

Thuy's makeup artist did a fabulous job on her face. Her hair was in a half-up half-down style with red roses in her hair. Her custom designed wedding dress was a V-neck mermaid style, that showed off her curves and sexy cleavage just a tad.

"Are you ready, ma'am?" The wedding planner handed Thuy, a bouquet of red roses.

"Oh yes." Thuy was filled with excitement. "I've been ready for a long time."

The wedding planner led Thuy out of the room and into the area on the beach where the wedding was gonna take place.

"Just follow the flower girls, they'll lead you to the altar, where your handsome groom will be waiting." She instructed.

"Alright." Thuy said.

The wedding planner pointed at the two flower girls holding their straw baskets filled with red rose petals. The wedding planner timed everything just right, before she gave the flower girls their cues.

"Ready, set, go!"

The flower girls walked ahead of Thuy leaving behind them a trail of red rose petals. When the song *All My Life* by *KC and Jo-Jo* started to play, the wedding planner signaled for Thuy, to follow the flower girl's trail.

It seemed like a long walk, but Thuy would walk all around the world and back three times to get to her man. There Macal, stood at the altar waiting on her, looking sexy and dashing in his sharp tux. When Thuy finally reached the altar, she and Macal were lost in each other's eyes.

There stood the minister ready to perform the ceremony. "We are gathered here today to witness and celebrate the union of Macal Jordy Kilborn and Thuy Mackenzie Ellis in marriage. Through their time together, they have come to realize that their hopes and dreams are more attainable and meaningful when joined as one by love, commitment and mutual support."

The minister continued. "Macal and Thuy, today you choose each other to begin your lives together. For the days that follow, you will choose each other over and over again in the privacy of your hearts. Let your love and friendship guide you to learn and grow together. Experience the wonders of the world, through your partnership, triumph and challenges in your path. With the comfort of loving arms, may you always find a safe place to call home."

A cute little boy who was the ring bearer held the rings that were lying on top of the satin pillow. "Now we will present the rings and exchange vows." The minister said.

Macal put the ring on Thuy's finger and recited his vows. "With this ring I thee wed. I Macal, take you Thuy, to be my lawfully wedded wife. To have and to hold, to love and cherish, through joy and sorrow, sickness and health, for better or worse, for richer or poorer, from this day forward, till death do us part."

Thuy, put the ring on Macal's finger and recited her vows. "With this ring I thee wed. I Thuy, take you Macal, to be my lawfully wedded husband. To have and to hold, to love and cherish, through joy and sorrow, sickness and health, for better or worse, for richer or poorer, from this day forward, till death do us part."

The minister then stated. "If they are no objections you may now kiss the bride."

He didn't have to tell Macal twice. He pulled Thuy into his arms and kissed her like he hadn't seen her in years. "I now present Mr. and Mrs. Macal Jordy Kilborn."

"Oh, my God! We're married!" Thuy cheered.

"Yes, we are baby!" Macal cheered and spun Thuy around in his arms with joy.

"Now that you're my husband what should we do next Mr. Kilborn?" Thuy asked.

"Well, now that you're my wife Mrs. Kilborn we have a lot of things to do." Macal said.

"Like what husband of mine?"

"Well, wife of mine. During our two week honeymoon, which will give Tylisha plenty of time to decorate our new mansion. For starters we'll be checking out this lovely city and its sights and casinos."

"Grandma Doris and Gladys gave us some great tips." Thuy said.

"Then we'll stop in Paris, The City of Love. Afterwards it's off to Barbados, but before we do any of that we have something very important to do."

"What's that?"

"Go to our honeymoon suite and consummate our marriage."

"You're right that is very important." Thuy agreed.

Macal and Thuy walked arm and arm to their suite while everyone took pictures and wished them congratulations. When they reached the floor that their suite was on Macal, carried Thuy, the rest of the way.

"This is gonna be great!" Thuy was on cloud nine. "Making love to my wonderful husband."

"Mmm, I can taste that sweet pussy already." Macal said as he opened the door to the suite.

 Macal laid Thuy on the bed and climbed on top of her. Her pussy was getting wetter by the second as they helped each other undress and get ready to fuck for the first time as husband and wife. Their fully nude bodies joined together.

"It doesn't get any better than this." Those were Thuy's last words before Macal entered the now Mrs. Thuy Mackenzie Ellis-Kilborn's pussy and she let out a loud moan.

Macal felt Thuy's powerful orgasm throughout his dick and grunted out. "You're right, baby. It doesn't get any better than this!"

Addicted to the Drama 2

Chapter 38

Eighteen Months Later

"Thuy, calm your ass down!" Macal yelled and ducked for cover at the flying objects aimed for his head, courtesy of a highly pissed off Thuy in the living room of their newly built mansion, where Jeromy's place of residence once stood.

"Your nasty ass is still fucking that bitch!" Thuy yelled with jealous rage and threw a cup at Macal.

"Girl, quit throwing shit at me."

Thuy ignored Macal by throwing a remote control at him. "Nasty motherfucker."

Thuy was about to grab another object to throw, but Macal charged in her direction to restrain her.

"I don't know what the fuck you talking about." Macal lied as usual.

"You don't think I know what the fuck your dick looks like nigga." Thuy struggled to get free from Macal's strong restraining grasp.

"Thotlette showed me the pictures on her phone when I was getting my hair done today." Thotlette was Thuy's derogatory pet name for Lolette and it caught on with her lifelong crew. For the past eighteen months Macal and Thuy's marriage has been a drama filled roller-coaster. One-minute things were great. Then the next minute, Macal's affairs came to light. Afterwards Macal and Thuy, had a big fight and then they made up. Of course, there was occasional altercations with Macal's side bitches especially the main one Lolette and the cycle kept repeating itself.

"She must've saved the picture a while back." Macal stuck with the lie.

"Cut the fucking shit nigga." Thuy screamed in his face. "Nigga I'm sick of your shit! Fucking all these bitches behind my back and that ringleader hoe Lolette, embarrassing me and shit. Do you want me to go crazy? Do you like it when I lose my motherfucking mind?"

Macal stood there in silence not knowing what to say which infuriated Thuy even further. She then started smacking Macal across the head repeatedly.

"Huh, nigga—huh!" Thuy kept smacking his head. "Is that it nigga? You like seeing me go crazy up in here?"

Macal grabbed Thuy's wrists to stop her from hitting him. "Girl you need to get a hold of yourself!"

"Nigga I don't need to get a hold of shit."

"Baby don't let Lolet—"

"Nigga don't motherfucking baby me! Your ass ain't gonna—"

"I don't know what the fuck she told you. Her ass is lying!"

****

Two Hours Later

In the king size bed in the master bedroom Macal had Thuy's legs spread eagle beating up the pussy for about ten more minutes before dumping his load deep inside her. He rolled off of Thuy and pulled her in his arms. The two laid in silence in their makeup sex after-glow.

"Macal, I'm scared." Thuy broke the silence.

"Scared of what, baby?" Macal stroked her hair.

"I'm scared I'm gonna lose you." Thuy's eyes started to water. "I love you so much and I don't wanna lose you. Especially to the likes of Thotlette."

Macal wiped Thuy's tears away from her cheeks and kissed her. "Baby, you have nothing to worry about. I'm not going any-where." He held her in his arms tighter. "You know, I love you."

"If you love me so much, why do you need all those bitches on your dick? Am I enough for you?" Thuy asked with sadness.

"Baby, I'm sorry. I'll try to do better. I wanna do better." Macal pleaded in his sweet sexy panty-wetting voice.

"You know I had to stomp that hoe again after she showed me

182

those pictures, right?"

"I had a feeling you did." The fucked up married couple shared a laugh.

Thuy laid her head on Macal's chest to hear his heartbeat. "I want this marriage to work."

"Me too." Macal kissed Thuy's head.

"You realize in order for this to work, you need to keep your dick out of those hoes and get Thotlette under control." Thuy said.

"Done." Macal said as he caressed Thuy's body. "Now no more worries, go to sleep. We have a long, busy day tomorrow."

"Tylisha and Enzo's wedding at the Commerce Club." Thuy said. "I'm so happy for them."

"Me too."

"You need to get some rest, too. You're walking Tylisha down the aisle."

"Exactly."

Jamila

Chapter 39

"You look fabulous." Ligia said when she finished helping Tylisha put on her wedding dress, that hugged her curves, with her hair in a bun.

"Thanks, Ligia, so do you." Tylisha complimented Ligia's lavender dress with her medium length curly afro pulled back.

"Look at my, baby girl." Doris said as she entered the dressing room.

"Grandma Doris!" Tylisha cheered and hugged her beloved grandmother.

"My little girl is marrying the man of her dreams." Doris said with pride and joy. "You look beautiful."

"I have my maid of honor to thank." Tylisha pointed at Ligia.

"Hi Mrs. Blair." Ligia hugged Doris.

"Hi sweetheart. Thanks for fixing up my baby." Doris said.

"I'll admit it's a little taboo to be the maid of honor at my ex-husband's wedding, but Tylisha asked me." Ligia appreciated Tylisha's support during her long difficult fight against cancer.

There was no way Ligia could pay Tylisha back but agreeing to be her maid of honor was a start.

"When is your next treatment?" Doris asked Ligia.

"In about three weeks. It's hard, but it gets better day by day." Ligia said.

"That's right." Doris nodded and put her arms around Ligia. "You just keep fighting. Don't give up, baby."

"I won't Mrs. Blair. Besides I can't if I wanted to. Your granddaughter, won't let me." Ligia joked but was serious.

"That's right!" Tylisha declared and the ladies laughed.

****

The wedding was a beautiful ceremony. Amery sung *Happily Ever After* by Case. To add more to the taboo wedding party Vax was Enzo's best man. Macal, walked Tylisha down the aisle. Everything was perfect. It had everything Tylisha wanted. Mainly because she'd decorated it.

After the wedding the reception was in full swing. Congratulating the newlyweds. The kids officially welcomed their now step-parents and step-siblings.

Now it was time for the dance. Macal took Tylisha by the hand and escorted her to the middle of the dancefloor. All eyes were on them.

"I have a special surprise for you." Macal said to Tylisha.

"What's that?" Tylisha asked smiling.

"Just listen." The siblings began to ballroom dance to the sounds of the piano music. As the song played Tylisha noticed the tunes were slightly familiar.

Tylisha got to thinking. *Wait a minute, this almost sounds like—*

Out of nowhere, Macal, busted out with the first verse of *Just a Friend* by *Biz Markie*.

Tylisha busted out laughing. "No, you didn't!" She started singing along with Macal.

After they finished singing their song, the guests gave them a round of applause. Enzo cut in to dance with Tylisha to the song *Here and Now* by *Luther Vandross*.

"Look at all the love on this joyous occasion." Thuy smiled with admiration at Enzo and Tylisha, with Macal's arms wrapped around her.

"They are so happy. Just like me and my Sam here." Vida said, kissing her husband.

"Yeah Mr. and Mrs. Samuel Ellis Jr. Who didn't tell nobody they asses eloped." Thuy referred to Sam and Vida's vacation to Hawaii and coming back as newlyweds.

"Yeah just sprung it on us." Macal joined in.

"That was six months ago little cuz." Sam said. "Don't you think you should let it go?"

"Besides y'all eloped too." Vida defended.

"At least we told y'all and threw a party before we left." Thuy said.

"At the last minute." Sam said.

"Whatever!" Thuy shot back.

"Anyway, how are you guys doing?" Vida asked.

"Better than ever." Macal answered and planted a kiss on Thuy. "Isn't that right, baby?"

"Right baby." Thuy blushed.

"I heard Green Safe is doing well on the stock market. Congrats to you both." Sam said.

"Thanks. We couldn't have done it without you." It was Thuy's idea to make Sam the spokesperson of Green Safe.

"Awe y'all are just saying that." Sam was being modest.

"It's true, baby. You look so sexy in that commercial." Vida gushed. "This is a nice wedding. Too bad Bryn couldn't be here."

"Yeah. He had to go to Phoenix, because his brother was having surgery." Thuy said.

"Let's congratulate the happy couple again." Thuy said.

"Let's." Vida said.

She, Thuy and Sam walked over to the newlyweds. Macal stayed behind to reply to a text message from this morning. Or rather a busted open pussy picture.

Macal: You got a pretty pussy baby!
Lolette: About time your ass responded nigga!

This bitch better be lucky the pussy is good, and she can suck dick like a pro! Macal rolled his eyes and sent a reply.

Macal: Whatever! Just be ready to fuck when I come over first thing tomorrow.
Lolette: Can't wait!

Jamila

Chapter 40

"How did we do, Aunt Naomi?" Fallon asked looking through the paperwork in the visiting room.

Fallon knew when she left Wadley she needed to build a nest egg and the divorce settlement was a great startup capital for her art dealing business. Also, Naomi bought a small portion of the cosmetic company she used to work for before she retired.

"Our profits increased by five percent since the last quarter." Naomi reported. "Those pieces you sold to the museum in New York was worth ten million dollars combined."

"Good—good!" Fallon nodded. "Marco came to see me two days ago to discuss his latest project."

"How's that going?"

"He should be finished by the end of the week." Fallon wrote down a phone number and gave it to Naomi. "He'll be expecting a call from you."

"Alright." Naomi put the number in her purse and handed Fallon a picture. "Doris sent me this."

"Tylisha and Enzo look so beautiful and happy." Fallon smiled at the wedding picture. "Where did they go for their honeymoon?"

"Bora Bora." Naomi answered.

"I'll make sure to have this portrait done before Tylisha's next visit." Fallon said.

Now that all the business was taken care of Naomi needed to know about the wellbeing of her niece and de facto daughter. "How are you?"

"I'm making it, trying to keep busy." Fallon answered. "How are things with you and Park?"

"Amazing!" Naomi answered glowing. "We visited his daughter and his grandchildren last week. We had a great time."

"Hey, Fallon." Rita approached their table and greeted.

"Rita, baby." Fallon hugged her mentee who had shown great promise with her artwork. "How you, doing?"

"Great, hi Miss Naomi!" Rita greeted.

"Hey, sweetheart." Naomi greeted back.

"Today is her birthday." Fallon pointed at Rita. "She's twenty-one now."

"Oh." Naomi pulled out her famous red velvet cake and peanut butter fingers. "That's why you had me bake all of this."

"Yeah!" Fallon confessed with a giggle.

"Happy birthday, Rita." Naomi said.

"Thank you so much!" Rita was full of joy.

"Come on Aunt Naomi!" Fallon cheered with excitement, while pulling Rita out of the visiting room.

"Where are we going?" Naomi was right on their tail.

Fallon frantically searched for the correct room and turned on the light. "Surprise! Happy birthday, Rita!" Everyone cheered.

Rita was blown away by the decorations, balloons, presents, snacks including Aunt Naomi's addition she placed on the table. "Wow, y'all did all of this for me?"

"Yes, baby girl." Chester gave his daughter a birthday hug and kiss.

"Daddy!"

"You're the birthday girl. You get the first bite." Naomi said, handing Rita a plate with a slice of cake and a peanut butter finger.

Rita took a bite out of her treats and fell in love with the taste. "This is great! Thanks Naomi."

"Now that you're twenty-one. Here you go. This wasn't easy to make happen." Fallon handed Rita a bottle of wine wrapped in a pink bow.

"Thanks Fallon." Rita smiled.

"The finest from, Paris." Fallon said.

"Oh, I feel so fancy and bougie." Rita joked, giggling.

"Maybe one day we'll take that trip to Paris together." Fallon said.

"I'd like that." Rita said, hugging her surrogate mom.

This turned out to be the best birthday in Rita's life. The love from her father, Fallon and Naomi. The friends she made, and the staff were very nice to her. Everybody in that party showed her more love in one day than that bitch of a mother of hers did in her whole life.

190

Addicted to the Drama 2

The party was over, Naomi went on her way home. Fallon volunteered to cleanup and Chester helped her.

"This was a great thing you did." Chester said to Fallon.

"Thanks Chester, Rita deserves it." Fallon said.

"Seeing my little girl smile is what I live for." Chester cleared off the table.

"That's sweet." Seeing the way Chester showed unconditional love for his daughter melted Fallon's heart. Not a day went by that she wished she had that fatherly love growing up.

The two gathered up the last of the trash and put it in the garbage bags. Chester tied the bags up and set them aside for the staff to throw out in the morning.

After all this time admiring Fallon from afar and concealing his desires for her. It was time for Chester to man up and get his woman.

"Fallon, I just wanna say that you're an amazing, wonderful, beautiful woman. Thanks for being a great role model to my daughter. What I'm trying to say is—uh—well"

"Daddy likes you and wants to ask you out!" Rita put Chester out of his misery, while peeking through the doorway.

She had a good feeling her father had a thing for Fallon but was too shy to admit it. Rita thought it was cute watching her daddy acting all shy around a woman he liked.

"Girl, get out of grown folks business." Chester playfully chastised.

"Sorry daddy, but you needed help." On that note Rita headed for her room.

"Tsk—tsk—tsk!" Fallon shook her head at Chester. "Your own daughter had to hook you up huh?"

Chester chuckled with embarrassment. "Maybe I didn't do a good job hiding my feelings."

To be honest, Fallon, had a deeply hidden desire for Chester as well. Playing with her clit in the shower wasn't cutting it anymore. She needed the real thing. However, considering her history with the opposite gender Fallon had to play it cool.

"Chester, you seem like a nice guy and I would love to go out with you, but I'm not sure if it'll work." Fallon looked around the

Jamila

room and back to Chester. "As you can see I have some major issues to deal with."

Chester smiled and rubbed Fallon's cheek. "You know what they say. Where there's a will there's a way." *What the fuck.* Throwing caution out the window Chester surprised Fallon, by pulling her into his arms and sticking his tongue in her mouth.

Fallon wasn't expecting this. She was confused, but not confused enough to stop Chester's kiss. His lips felt so good. His warm mouth and strong tongue made Fallon picture how great his head game would be.

Still pressed against his body Fallon, felt his long thick hard-on through his pants. When Chester, grabbed her juicy ass just right, Fallon broke the kiss. Not because she wanted the make out session to end, but she knew in about one more minute she would've let Chester bend her over that table and knock the cobwebs out of her pussy.

"Maybe we should take this slow." Fallon panted.

"I can respect that." Chester said and planted a quick kiss on Fallon's lips. "As long as we're moving we good."

Chapter 41

"You gonna take good care of my baby, right?" Ms. Miller asked Thuy during their business lunch at the Lenox Square food court.

The meeting was to discuss her son Craig's debut in the NFL.

"Yes, I will Ms. Miller." Thuy answered.

"We know you the best." Ms. Miller said.

"Thank you." Thuy blushed. "Also, my husband and I are founders of Green Safe Services. I suggest your son enroll in order to help him properly manage his salary. We all know he can't play football forever, so he needs to prepare for a strong stable financial future."

Ms. Miller turned to her only child. "She makes a good point baby."

"Yes momma." Craig nodded and turned to Thuy. "Alright, I'll sign with you and do the Green Safe thing."

"Perfect." Thuy smiled, handing Craig the contracts. "Here are the contracts. Look over it, if you have any questions, feel free to give me a call. I'll be in touch, okay."

"Yes ma'am." Craig shook her hand.

"Thank you so much, Mrs. Kilborn." Ms. Miller shook Thuy's hand.

"No thanks needed. Just doing my job." Thuy said.

After the meeting ended Thuy, dropped in at Bloomingdale's and went over to the shoe department. She browsed through the shoes to see if she saw anything she liked. During her search she came across a pair of gold sandals. She was about to grab them but froze in shock. She was facing the direction of a man she'd wished to forget. *Connor Hale.*

"What the fuck." She mumbled under her breath.

****

1996

Thuy, Vida and Bryn were at their school lockers, getting ready to go home.

"What y'all got planned after school?" Thuy asked her friends.

"I gotta go to my sister's house to babysit my nephews." Vida answered. "Y'all wanna join me?"

"Sure." Bryn said.

"I'll join you." Thuy said. "My momma gotta work late anyway."

Thuy was about to say something else, but she was pushed very hard. She would've hit the floor if Bryn hadn't caught her in time. Thuy turned around to see who the asshole or bitch was, who'd signed their own death warrant. The perpetrator was a bitch named, Shandi Russell, who Thuy's ex-boyfriend left her for, along with her little friends, licking their forever dick-sucking chops.

"Bitch, what the fuck is your problem?" Thuy was in no mood for the bullshit.

"Your ass ain't slick hoe." Shandi got in Thuy's face. "I heard you trying to fuck my man again. I don't appreciate that shit, bitch!"

Having an unfair reputation as the school's slut was fucking with Thuy deep inside. If she didn't have Bryn and Vida she didn't know how she'd make it through.

"Shandi, go on somewhere." Bryn waved her off. "Your ass look stupid trying to show out in front of your bitch pack."

"Nigga shut your faggot ass up." Shandi snapped at Bryn before turning her jealous fury back on Thuy. "Everybody knows your ass is a hoe, if you think you'll get Connor again, you are dead ass motherfucking wrong!"

"Bitch you can have Connor's two-minute ass." Thuy's retort made Shandi's friends laugh their heads off. She made that two-minute comment to be justifiably spiteful.

Shandi's ego must've been bruised, because she ended up making the biggest mistake of her life by slapping Thuy's face. In retaliation Thuy punched Shandi dead in her nose, jacked her up, and slammed her body against the lockers. Thuy beat the shit out of that stuck up trick. The fight didn't fix Thuy's reputation, but everybody learned to never fuck with Thuy again.

Addicted to the Drama 2

****

"Well—well—well, Thuy Ellis!" Connor walked up on Thuy and greeted.

Thuy would've been left, but her feet weren't moving while she had her flashback.

"Connor." Thuy kept her cool.

"Still looking lovely and sexy as ever." Connor flashed his charming smile. "It's great to see, you."

"Yeah thanks." Thuy said with nonchalance. "I wish I could say the same with your fuck nigga ass. Good day and kick rocks." Thuy responded with cold-blooded, rudeness as she prepared to leave. Fuck those shoes she wanted to buy. The sight of that nigga fucked up her whole shopping experience.

Thuy tried to find the exit, but Connor caught up with her, and blocked her path. "Whoa, what the fuck was that about?"

Is this nigga, serious? "You gotta be shitting me motherfucker. After taking my virginity you dumped me for that stuck up bitch and told the whole world what a great fuck I was after promising me, you wouldn't. Causing the whole school to think, I would jump on any dick in a heartbeat including your rapist buddy, Levi!" Thuy reminded Connor of his crimes against her. "You know what, get the fuck out of my face."

Shit, I really was an asshole back in the day. Connor saw Thuy walk off in a huff. He didn't realize how bad he'd hurt this woman. Are men really that selfish about their wants, needs and pleasures, to the point that they don't give two fucks about the women they dog out along the way? Connor had to make it right, but he didn't know how. All he could do was apologize to Thuy and set things right.

"Wait a minute." Connor caught up with Thuy again. "I'm sorry about what happened between us. I was a young, ignorant, selfish bastard. I know it's not an excuse. I didn't mean to hurt you. Really, I didn't, but there's something you need to know."

"What?"

"You're right, I did some fucked up shit to you, but I never

195

spoke a word about you to Levi." Connor said.

Huh? Thuy shook her head. "What are you talking about?"

"I was never friends with that nigga."

"Excuse me?"

"No, I couldn't stand that nigga!"

"That night he attacked me. He said you told him about me."

"That nigga lied." Connor insisted. "His ass always held a grudge against me ever since me and my boys jumped his pussy ass."

"Why did y'all jump him?" Thuy asked.

"Before you came in the picture, Levi, tried to step to a friend of my homebody's girl. When she wouldn't fuck him, he slapped her and pushed her out of his car. We found him and stomped that ass." Connor explained.

This new information was too much for Thuy. She couldn't think straight. She had to get out of there and clear her head.

"My head is spinning like crazy. If you didn't tell Levi about me, who did?"

"I don't know, but I know it wasn't me." Connor said. "I'm sorry about everything that happened to you."

Thuy, didn't know what to believe or think. Maybe Connor was telling the truth. Why would he lie now? He was very apologetic. If he could apologize so could she.

"Connor I'm sorry about my attitude. I should've handled the situation better. It was good seeing you again, I'm glad you're well. Take care."

"Apology accepted." Connor hugged, Thuy. "Even though I don't really deserve one."

"We're adults now and holding grudges is childish. Also, people do change."

"Some for better and some for worse."

"You got that right."

Chapter 42

In the visiting room of the DeKalb County correctional facility, there sat a chestnut brown-skinned woman, wearing an all black Chanel pantsuit, with her long, curly, dark honey blonde lace front wig on point. She had the body of a twenty-one-year old, but the minor wrinkles around her dark brown bedroom eyes gave away her advanced age. She patiently waited for the inmate she was there to visit to approach her table and there he was.

"Hey girl." Jeromy greeted his ally, who he referred to as Lady-T by kissing her hand.

Jeromy was captivated by this woman's beauty and boss presence. He noticed some of his fellow inmates, male visitors, and even a few male correctional officers checking out the sexy cougar. Jeromy wondered if she was turning heads now, the nigga's necks must've been broken during her days of prime in the 1980s and 1990s.

"Hey." Lady-T blushed at Jeromy's charm. "How are you holding up in here?"

"Making it."

"That's all we can do, right?" Lady-T replied. "DeDe still putting money on your books?"

"Yes, that dumb ugly hoe is." Jeromy laughed at how gullible, desperate, and pathetic DeDe was.

Jeromy nearly pissed in his drawers, when Lady-T shared with him how Thuy, laid out that ugly hoe at Enzo's birthday party.

"Everything is all set." Lady-T reported.

"Good." Jeromy said with relief. "I was getting impatient."

"Good things come to those who wait."

"My ass been waiting long enough." Jeromy wanted Thuy to get hers ASAP, but he understood why he had to play by time's rules, in order for this shit to work.

He was lucky to have Lady-T by his side. Who knew he'd run across someone who was interested in helping him get revenge on Thuy and Macal. Who also had ideas and amazing resources of her own.

Jamila

"What you got for me?" Jeromy asked.

"Everyone is doing their part, right now." Lady-T said. "It wasn't hard. Thuy's husband can't seem to stay out of outside pussy."

"Good for her ass." Jeromy chuckled at his ex's marital issues.

"Just like his daddy." Lady-T mumbled under her breath.

"What was that?"

"Excuse me. I burped." Lady-T lied. "Remember to keep DeDe pacified and the less she knows the better. The last thing I need is some ignorant, ugly ass, ratchet, hood-rat bitch ruining my plans."

"Gotcha."

"If you have any ideas or need anything let me know." Lady-T got out of her seat ending the visit.

"Cool." Jeromy hugged Lady-T, deeply inhaling the aroma of her expensive floral scented perfume. "Lady-T, before you go I gotta ask you something."

"I'm all ears."

"We've been working together for some time and you know my reasons. My question is what's in it for you?"

Lady-T flashed a sexy, wicked grin and answered with a voice as cold as ice. "Justice and collecting my debts."

Chapter 43

The sun was setting on the home of Vida and Sam. Sam had a race in Italy. Vida felt lonely, so she invited her two BFFs over for drinks on the patio, enjoying the weather, and the beautiful sunset. They had frozen margaritas, Scorpion Bowls and now Vida's world famous Bahama mamas.

Vida looked over at Thuy, noticing she was nowhere near finished with her drink. Usually, Thuy, would be asking for a refill by now. "What's wrong, Thuy? Your glass is still full."

"What?" Thuy looked at her glass and took a sip. "Oh, sorry, I was a little distracted."

"Distracted by what?" Bryn asked. "Work?"

"No." Thuy shook her head.

"You and Macal, having problems again?" Vida guessed.

"No." Thuy shook her head again.

"We gotta tear Thotlette a new one again." Vida guessed again.

"Close, but still no." Thuy pointed at Vida and finished her drink.

"How the fuck is that close?" Bryn blurted out.

"It's Connor." Ever since Thuy's run in with Connor she'd been doing the math in her head wondering why the fuck, every time she tried to add two plus two together, it equaled five, ten, infinity or some fucked up number that doesn't exist, like eleventy-twelve.

"Connor." Vida and Bryn exclaimed.

"Yes, Connor." Thuy confirmed. "I ran into him at Lenox Square, after my meeting with a client."

"What was his ass talking about?" Bryn rolled his eyes. "I hope you cussed his ass out."

"You know I did." Thuy grinned. "Afterwards, he apologized for dogging me out and all that other shit, but he also said something very interesting."

"What did he say?" Vida asked.

"Remember my attack, when Levi said Connor told him about me?" Thuy asked.

"Yeah." Vida said.

"Connor said he never told Levi about me." Thuy said. "In fact, they were never friends. They hated each other."

"Excuse me?" Bryn gulped his drink.

"My words exactly." Thuy said. "I don't know. Connor could've changed and maybe he's telling the truth."

"I think Connor, is telling the truth." Vida said.

"You do?" Thuy asked.

"Yeah. It's coming back to me." Vida gathered her memory. "One day I took my nephews out for ice cream. Across the street a fight broke out. Actually, it was more of a beat down than a fight. The dude who was jumped on was, Levi and one of the guys that was beating his ass was, Connor."

"Oh shit." Thuy gasped surprised. "Connor told me about that fight. They jumped on Levi, because he slapped and threw a chick they knew out of his car."

Bryn's memory was starting to go into overdrive as well. "Now that I think about it, I never saw Connor and Levi hang out together. Whenever they passed each other in the hallway, they never spoke a word to each other."

"So, Connor is telling the truth?" Thuy concluded.

"That's what it looks like." Bryn nodded in agreement.

"That means somebody else told Levi about you." Vida said.

"Obviously, but who could it be." Thuy wondered.

"Whoever it was knew about your first time with Connor and your unfair reputation." Bryn hypothesized.

"That could be anybody." Thuy shrugged.

"True that." Then Bryn asked the multi-million-dollar question. "But how many of those people knew what Levi was capable of."

Addicted to the Drama 2

Chapter 44

Thuy and Macal, were on a double date with Enzo and Tylisha. The occasion was more like a late wedding present for Enzo and Tylisha. Thuy and Macal, treated them to the concert and the after party. They had a great time and now they were in the parking lot heading towards their vehicle.

"That concert was off the chain." Tylisha cheered with Enzo's arms around her. "And that after party was wild and crazy!"

"Yep. Free VIP treatment all the way!" Enzo said.

"That's the best kind." Tylisha said. "Thanks for making it happen, Macal and Thuy."

"It was our pleasure." Macal said. "But my baby here, deserves most of the credit." He kissed Thuy.

"How did you make this happen, Thuy?" Enzo asked.

"What can I say? I'm just smooth like that." Thuy bragged with cockiness. "And the lead singer of the opening act is the nephew of my client's fiancée."

"My baby got juice." Macal said.

"Awe Macal, you're the greatest." Thuy said.

"I know." Macal's ego was off the charts.

"Conceited ass nigga." Thuy cut her eyes at Macal. "How's married life?" She asked the newlyweds.

"So far, so good." Tylisha said.

"Being married to this woman is the best thing ever." Enzo said, feeling like the luckiest man in the world.

"Awe Enzo. You're just saying that, because it's completely true." Tylisha boasted with a fake modest demeanor.

"I see being conceited runs in the family." Enzo whispered to Thuy.

"I know, right." Thuy agreed with Enzo.

"It's getting late and my black ass is hungry. Where y'all wanna eat?" Macal asked.

"I don't know." Tylisha shrugged. "I'm not picky."

"As long as it's not Waffle House or Ihop. Those places are so cliché. No imagination whatsoever." Thuy said. "Let's stop at the

201

first place we run into that's still open."

"Fine with me." Enzo said, and everyone nodded in agreement.

The four finally found the car and stopped dead in their tracks when they saw a familiar yet unwelcomed person sitting on the hood of the car. "Hey Macal!"

"Lolette, what the fuck are you doing here sitting on my ride?" Macal snapped.

"Her ass is like a fucking cockroach." Thuy rolled her eyes.

"I heard that, Thuy, I don't appreciate that shit." Lolette, let it be known, that she didn't like Thuy's insult.

"Who gives a fuck what you appreciate, Thotlette?" Thuy tried to roll up on Lolette, but Tylisha grabbed her wrist stopping her.

"Lolette, will you please leave. We don't want any trouble." Enzo tried to play peacemaker.

Lolette, got off of the hood of the car. "I was about to leave anyway, but before I go. I have something to say first. I'm pregnant!"

"And?" Tylisha dismissed, like who gives a fuck.

"And—" Lolette mocked Tylisha's tone. "Macal's the daddy, that's all I wanted to say. Goodnight everyone."

After dropping the baby bomb, Lolette left the two couples with confused looks on their faces.

"Uh—what did she just say?" Enzo was the first to speak.

"I think she said something about being pregnant." Tylisha said.

"Yeah, she said that, but she also said something else crazy." Enzo added on.

"I think she said Macal, was the father." Tylisha said.

Enzo and Tylisha glanced over at Macal and Thuy. Macal was still in disbelief, about what he'd just heard, and Thuy stood there with no emotion on her face.

Macal couldn't believe Lolette, was pregnant with his baby. This shit couldn't be happening. He didn't know what to do. He'd figure that out later, but first he had to explain himself to, Thuy.

"Listen, baby, I'm sorry. I didn't—"

Thuy, slapped the hell out of Macal, and screamed to the sky with rage. "Nigga, you got that bitch pregnant! How the fuck could you do this to me." Tears flowed from her eyes nonstop. "You said, you was done with that hoe and you still fucking her. You ain't shit, nigga!"

"Baby, let me explain!" Macal pleaded.

"Explain what? There ain't shit to explain!" Thuy hit Macal again. "Shit—shit—shit!" Thuy kept hitting Macal repeatedly, Tylisha and Enzo struggled to get her off of him.

****

"Shit—shit—shit!" Lolette, mocked as she witnessed the anger filled spectacle from afar.

"I'm assuming you told them?" The man on the other end of the phone said.

"Yes, the fuck I did and she's losing her fucking mind." Lolette, replied with delight.

"I wish I could be there to see that shit." The mystery man chuckled. "Now, get that sexy good pussy having ass over here, so I can get you pregnant for real."

Jamila

Chapter 45

At the dealership, Thuy, was hard at work in her office. Ever since the news of Lolette's baby came out the only thing, keeping Thuy from going insane and brutally murdering Macal was work.

Thuy was looking through some contracts, when she heard a knock at the door. "Come in."

Tori, entered the office with two bags from Popeye's. "Hey girl. How you holding up?"

"Shit! I have no clue."

"Have you and Macal, talked?"

"Other than, about Green Safe, nope. I'm just trying to focus on my work, trying not to think about my husband getting his main hoe pregnant."

"I know it doesn't take the pain way, but I got you this." Tori placed the Popeye's bag on the table.

"Popeye's, you shouldn't have." Thuy jumped up and down with joy, hugging her sister. "Popeye's does help a little."

"What are your plans?" Tori took her seat and the ladies at their lunch.

"Plans, what the fuck are those?" Thuy sarcastically scoffed. "To be honest, I don't know why the fuck my life is so crazy. It seems like everywhere I go drama seems to follow me."

"Let me ask you this. Do you still love, Macal?"

"Of course, I love him, but I don't know how much I can take. The cheating, the lies, the secrets and now a baby with another woman." Thuy sighed in defeat.

Minus the cheating Macal, was the perfect husband. He loved, Thuy, unconditionally. He supports her. Makes her feel special. Protects her, and he never tried to kill her like Jeromy did. That was a plus. How in the fuck was, Thuy, gonna deal with Macal's latest fuck up?

"I don't mean to offend you, but you know who you sound like, Momma." Tori said.

Being compared to her evil bitch stepmother made Thuy's skin crawl, but she understood the connection. "Tori, I know Mycha is your mother, but she gave me hell. If only she understood, I didn't ask to be born in this fucked up situation."

"I know you didn't." Tori said. "It was hard for momma to see you was innocent in all of this. The only thing she saw, was the man she loved, had betrayed her and she had to be constantly reminded about it every day."

"I didn't ask for this shit, but neither did she." Thuy realized.

"Momma loved daddy so much. In her own misguided way, she tried to hang onto him. She didn't wanna lose him. I'll admit she shouldn't have treated you like shit and Jet and I shouldn't have followed her lead." Tori sounded remorseful.

"I know. At least y'all apologized and we were able to rebuild our relationship."

"Momma, stayed with daddy, but she should've handled things differently." Tori took a bite out of her biscuit. "Maybe in a way you could learn from her mistakes."

"How?" Thuy grabbed another piece of chicken.

"She loved daddy, unconditionally. That's why she stayed, but she was wrong, for what she put you through and the bad examples she set." Tori explained. "Put it this way. You didn't deserve to be treated like a leper. Neither does Lolette's baby."

"What are you saying?" Thuy raised an eyebrow.

Tori continued. "Macal fucked up big time. We all can agree on that. If you do decide to stay, consider all the possibilities. That baby is gonna be a part of your lives. How would you handle it?"

Thuy sighed. "It's a lot to deal with. It'll be a lot easier if the mother wasn't a nasty, sleazy, bitch. I feel sorry for that baby. They gotta tell people that poor excuse of nature is their mother. What if I stay and Macal and I have kids of our own? Lolette's baby is gonna be their sibling and they have a right to have a healthy relationship. It's a lot to consider, one thing's for sure. As long as I'm around that baby will never know what it's like to be a family outcast."

Someone knocked on the door and let themselves in. "Mrs. Kilborn, I'm sorry to interrupt but a gentleman asked for you specifically to wait on him."

"This won't take long. I'll be right back." Thuy said to Tori, before leaving her office to see who the customer was in the show-room. To her surprise it was Connor with a beautiful young teenage girl who looked like she could be related him.

"Hello beautiful." Connor greeted.

"Hello Connor." Thuy greeted back more politely this time. "Who do we have here?" Thuy asked referring to Connor's teenage companion.

"This is my niece." Connor introduced. "She's going to Clark Atlanta University, she needs a safe dependable ride."

"Clark Atlanta? That's me and my two best friends' alma mater and one of them is a professor there." Thuy smiled. "What's your name sweetheart?"

"Argan Hale." The young lady answered.

"Nice to meet, you?" Thuy shook Argan's hand.

"She's nice and pretty, Uncle Connor." Thuy blushed at Argan's comment.

"I told you she was." Connor said. "I used to date this beautiful lady, but I was too selfish and immature to know what a good thing I had."

"What?" Argan replied.

"That's right." Connor confessed. "Your uncle was one of those low-down niggas, I warned you about. I hope this beautiful young woman has it in her heart to forgive me."

Thuy was really touched by this revelation. Connor was a changed man after all. "She forgives you." After accepting Connor's apology Thuy called for one of her salespeople. "Macy!"

"Yes, Mrs. Kilborn." Macy reported.

"I need you to show this lovely young lady our selections." Thuy instructed.

"Yes ma'am." Macy said. "Right this way young lady."

When they left Thuy took advantage of her moment alone with Connor.

"I do forgive you, I now know you're telling the truth about that night."

"I'm sorry that happened to you." Connor said with regret.

"The question now is who told Levi about me? Bryn and Vida

think it was a setup."

"That's trifling as hell." Connor said. "It's amazing the amount of hate in someone's heart can drive them to do some fucked up shit."

"They're some crazy motherfuckers out there." Thuy could definitely vouch for that after what she went through with Jeromy.

"You're right about that. That's why I'm divorced now."

"You're divorced?"

"Yep." Connor held up two fingers. "I chucked these deuces to that disloyal, undercover, ratchet bitch five years ago. Had to give her half my shit, but it was a small price to pay, to get her the fuck out my life."

"Why didn't it work out?" Thuy never in a million years thought Connor would ever get married. Surprise, surprise!

"Long story." Connor sighed. "I know you're married." He pointed at Thuy's wedding ring. "The fat rock and the new last name were dead giveaways."

"Yeah, I'm married." Thuy sounded unenthusiastic.

"Uh oh, trouble in paradise?" Connor guessed.

"You don't know the half of it."

"Uncle Connor! I found it, this is the car I want!" Argan cheered, pointing at a hot pink two door Audi.

Thuy and Connor went over to Argan. "Excellent choice." Thuy said.

Another sales person walked up to Thuy and said. "Excuse me. Your sister said she had to take off, but she said she'll call you later."

Thuy kicked herself for forgetting Tori was still in her office. "Alright thanks." She turned her attention back to her customers. "If you two will follow me into my office we'll get started with the paperwork."

Chapter 46

"How are things with you and Thuy?" Tylisha asked Macal, while they were sitting in the living room of his home.

"We're talking, and she hasn't called a divorce attorney yet." Macal sounded hopeful.

"Any progress is better than no progress." Tylisha said.

"Exactly. Anyway, thanks for not giving me a hard time about this and yelling at me." Macal said.

"Macal, if I yelled at you for every dumb, ass stupid thing you did, I'd lose my voice by now." Tylisha sighed, shaking her head. "Have you spoken with Lolette, about the baby?"

"No and it's not, because I'm avoiding her." Macal, wanted to make that very clear. "It's because, I can't get in touch with her."

Tylisha found that odd. "What do you mean?"

"I tried calling and texting her. She hasn't been home. She hasn't even popped up out of the blue." Macal said. "It's like she vanished off the face of the fucking earth."

"You mean to tell me these past three weeks, after dropping the baby bomb, Lolette, is nowhere to be found and you haven't heard a peep out of her?" Something about that didn't sit right with Tylisha.

"Strange isn't it."

"No shit!" Tylisha was trying to make sense of all of this, it was hard, but she had to try. "The night of the concert. Was that the first time you knew about the baby?"

"Yes." Macal answered. "I was just as surprised as y'all were. Lolette, never mentioned anything about being pregnant until that night."

"I see." *What the fuck is that bitch up to?* Tylisha thought.

She didn't know what the fuck Lolette, was trying to pull, but Tylisha was determined to find out.

Thuy walked downstairs with her luggage. "I'm ready to go."

"Where you going?" Tylisha asked.

"I'm going to L.A. for the USC versus Notre Dame game to check out the draft prospects." Thuy answered.

"Enjoy your trip and stay safe." Tylisha said, hugging Thuy.
"Thanks."

Macal walked over to Thuy to give her a hug. "Have a safe trip, baby." He kissed her on the lips.

"Thanks." Thuy opened the door to exit the house.

"I love you." Macal said.

"I love you, too." Thuy managed to say and went on her way.

****

On the plane, Thuy, was sitting comfortably in first class waiting for the plane to take off. She gazed out the window lost in her thoughts. She heard someone take a seat next to her. Curiosity made her look over to see who it was and her eyed widened.

"Connor!"

Connor looked over at Thuy, smiling. "Three times, are you following me?"

"Me, following you?" Thuy laughed. "Quite the contrary, I think you're following me."

"Uh huh." Connor responded. "Why you going to L.A.?"

"Business, you?"

"Going home and just in time. My alma mater is playing Notre Dame."

"You're kidding? That's the game I'm going too!" Thuy explained.

"This is a very small world." Connor said.

"Yeah." Thuy said. "I'm going to the game to check out draft prospects."

"I'm on the USC's Alumni committee. I'm sure I can help you out a bit." Connor offered.

"You'll do that for little ole me?" Thuy asked flashing those innocent eyes.

"Of course, it's the least I can do." Connor said. "That is if you don't mind keeping me company to the events?"

"Connor, I don't mind at all."

Addicted to the Drama 2

Chapter 47

Two Days Later

After weeks of Lolette, going ghost Macal, was finally able to get a hold of her. They agreed to meet at a restaurant, three blocks away from Six Flags. Lolette, was running thirty minutes late and Macal was getting impatient.

"What the fuck is taking her ass so long?" Macal, mumbled under his breath in frustration. He looked up and there was Lolette, standing before him. "Well it's about fucking time."

"Nice to see you too, nigga." Lolette was taken aback by Macal's rudeness and took a seat across the table from him. "The doctor's appointment took longer than I thought." Actually, she was telling the truth about her late doctor's appointment, that she filled her real baby daddy in on.

"How's the baby?"

"The baby is fine."

"Where the hell did you disappear to?" Macal, wanted to get to the bottom of this shit. "I've been trying to get a hold of your ass for three motherfucking weeks."

Lolette, let her eyes water a little bit. Preparing to put on the performance of a lifetime. "I had to get away to clear my head. Things have been crazy, I didn't mean to scare you." She sighed and kept on with her fake ass woe is me act. "I didn't think you cared about me or this baby. I didn't know what to do."

Being a sucker for damsels in distress Macal, held Lolette's hand for comfort and dried her tears with a napkin. "Lolette, it's gonna be okay. That's why I wanted to meet with you. To talk to about the baby and find a peaceful solution."

Lolette, snatched her hand away and threw a fit assuming what Macal's solution was. "I ain't getting no abortion. You can forget that shit, nigga!"

"Calm your ass down." Macal, said in a calming voice.

When it came to spontaneous, ghetto, outbursts Lolette,

Tylisha, and Thuy had a lot in common. Macal hated it when they did that shit.

"I'm not getting an abortion." Lolette reiterated.

"Nobody's asking you to get an abortion. I'd never ask that of you." Macal, wasn't trying to end up like his daddy.

He remembered what happened to Rufus when he tricked his main mistress into getting an abortion.

That wasn't the response, Lolette, was expecting. "You don't want me to get an abortion?"

"That's up to you. I'm not gonna ask you to get one or force you to make a decision."

"Okay." Lolette nodded.

"If you do decide to keep the baby, I'll be there for our child. You and the baby won't have to worry about a thing." Macal promised.

"Thank you." Lolette said with deep gratitude. "Why are you being cool about this?"

Macal, sighed and gave his answer. "You probably already know this, but when I was a kid my father was in a similar situation. Except, he had the balls to tell the woman to get an abortion."

"Yeah, I know all about that." Lolette said.

"I wanna be different." Macal said. "Yes, I had this baby on Thuy, but I'm trying to take responsibility and fix my marriage."

"I understand."

"I'll do my part, I trust you'll do yours."

"Absolutely."

"That means take care of yourself and the baby. Act like you got some sense, treat my wife with respect." Macal respectfully laid down the law.

"We good, as long as she don't try me."

"She won't." Macal assured. "She just needs time to adjust to all of this." Macal was interrupted by his phone's text notification. "Excuse me for a moment."

"Sure."

The text was from an unknown number with a picture attachment. Macal opened the message and there was a picture of Thuy, cuddled up in the corner with another man in a flirtatious way.

"What the fuck?" Macal was outraged.

"What's wrong?" Lolette asked with concern.

"I gotta go." Macal hopped out of his seat.

"Where?"

"No time to explain. I'll call you when I get back!" Macal, rushed out and on his way to find out what the fuck was going on with his wife and this unknown nigga.

Jamila

Chapter 48

Vax was taking Ligia to her doctor's appointment. They were singing along to *Me and My Girlfriend* by *Jay-Z* featuring *Beyoncé,* that was playing on the radio. The song was fitting, because Ligia could almost pass for Beyoncé, with her long curly Beeline honey blonde lace front wig. Also, like Jay-Z and Beyoncé, Vax was a grown man when Ligia was a teenager.

"I just love your voice." Vax said, leaning over to kiss Ligia.

"Thanks, and your rapping skills are pretty dope." Ligia complimented back. "Are you sure it's no bother taking me to the doctor?"

"It's no bother at all baby."

"Are you sure? Because you know I could've asked Tylisha to take me since she has the house to herself. With Enzo and the kids being gone and all." Ligia said.

"It's fine. I'm with you every step of the way." Vax said. "You are my ride or die."

"And vice versa." Ligia smiled. The next song to play on the radio was *Ryde or Die Chick* by *The Lox* featuring *Timbaland* and *Eve*. "Oh, how appropriate!" She laughed.

"I haven't heard this song in ages." Vax turned up the radio and the beautiful couple rapped along to the song.

Ligia stopped in the middle of Eve's verse when she saw something strange out the window.

"What's wrong, baby?" Vax wanted to know why Ligia stopped singing.

"I'm good."

"Are you sure?"

"It's cool, I thought I saw something."

"Saw what?"

"It's probably nothing." Ligia shook it off. "I thought I saw Milton back there."

"That's impossible." Vax said. "Milton is taking the kids out of town to visit family."

"Right, maybe my eyes are playing tricks on me." Ligia

dropped her suspicion and enjoy the car ride.

****

"When is daddy coming back?" Ayla asked Welton.

"I don't know, but he needs to hurry up." Welton said.

Welton and Ayla, were sitting outside in Milton's car waiting for him to come out of a hotel room, he stopped at so they could go on their trip. Welton and Ayla, enjoyed the fun times with their father. The only thing they didn't like, was when he had to make his 'stops'. They didn't understand why he had to make those stops.

The children continued to wait for their father. Ayla looked up and saw a tall muscular black man approaching the room Milton, was in doing whatever the fuck he was doing.

"Who's that?" Ayla asked.

Welton looked up and saw the dude Ayla was talking about. "How should I know?"

"It looks like he's going in the same room where daddy is."

Welton saw the unknown nigga open the door to the room. "You're right, he's going in the room."

****

"Bitch! Where the fuck is my money?" The unknown dude yelled in the skinny blonde woman's face. Looking like her pussy walls were condemned for demolition.

The hoe stuttered with fear of her pimp. All that came out of her mouth was. "I was—I—was—uh—trying—to—"

The pimp shut her up, with a hard pimp slap to the face. "Hoe don't talk unless I ask your dumb ass a fucking question! Now where the fuck is my money?"

The junkie whore didn't know what to say. Her not answering his question fast enough, made the pimp angrier and he pimp slapped her again.

"Bitch I asked you a fucking question! Where the fuck is my money? Your ass been out all motherfucking day, I ain't got a

216

fucking penny."

Milton tried to intervene when he got dressed. "Look man, I don't know what the fuck is going on."

"Nigga, ain't nobody talking to your ass." The pimp shut Milton down and focused back on his ivory coke-fiend whore. "Now where the fuck is my money?"

He surveyed the room and on the table, he saw evidence that cocaine was used. "You snorting my shit?" When he didn't get an answer, he flipped the table over. "Bitch you snorting my shit? You a dead bitch."

The pimp lifted his shirt and pulled out his Glock.

"Ah!" The drug addicted slut let out a blood curdling scream before the pimp proceeded to empty his clip throughout the room. *Pow! Pow! Pow!*

Jamila

Chapter 49

Game day was very exciting and thrilling. USC beat Notre Dame in overtime with a field goal. Connor's frat brothers were tailgating, they had the best barbeque and beer selections. The party didn't stop there. Thuy and Connor, where hanging out at a karaoke bar enjoying each other's company.

"I haven't had this much fun in a long time." Thuy giggled.

"I'm glad you enjoyed yourself." Connor smiled.

"I felt like I was in college again." Thuy took a shot of Don Julio Tequila. "And your frat brothers are very nice."

"They're a good bunch of guys." Connor said.

"That backup running back, you told me about. That boy is legit. Why in the hell ain't there any buzz about him?" Thuy asked.

"He's a freshman." Connor answered.

"Oh." Thuy nodded in agreement. "Well, I'm gonna keep a close eye on him. Good looking out Connor." The two toasted their shot glasses and took it to the head.

"Anytime, anytime."

"Since you already know how I make my money. How do you make yours?"

"I'm a real estate developer."

"Looks like you're doing a good job with that. Buying your niece cars and shit." Thuy teased.

"That's my baby, right there." Connor said with pride and joy. "The closest I have to a kid."

"You don't have any kids?"

"Nope." Connor answered. "I wanted to be a father so badly. One of the reasons I'm divorced."

"What happened with your marriage?"

"Long story."

"I have time." Thuy pressed for the dirt.

Connor let out a laugh. "Thuy, I noticed you were kind of dismissive about your marriage back at the dealership."

"Oh man." Thuy replied with annoyance and disgust. "I don't wanna talk about that nigga right now."

Jamila

"I'll make a deal with you."

"What kind of a deal?"

"You really wanna know about my bitch of an ex-wife?"

"Yes, I do."

"I'll give you all the details, under one condition."

"You name it."

"You return the favor."

My nosy ass walked into that one. But because, Thuy just had to know, she agreed to Connor's terms. "Deal."

Connor went on to discuss his disastrous marriage. He was in hellish matrimony for eight years. At first everything was good. He thought he'd found the perfect woman. Then she started living off him. Not doing shit with her life, except spending Connor's money on herself, her friends and secret side niggas. Just being an all-around, gold-digging, ratchet scandalous bitch.

The deal breaker was when she lied about having three miscarriages. It turned out she was having abortions behind Connor's back. All of her pregnancies, were results of her fucking around on him. She almost got away with it, had it not been for the fact that, the last abortion clinic she went to was across the street from the building Connor's company was setting up.

After Connor's story, Thuy, fulfilled her end of the bargain by filling Connor in on Macal and her marriage. When she was finished she grew silent in deep thought about what she should do next.

"Damn, baby girl." Connor caressed Thuy's cheek with care. "You don't deserve this shit."

"Neither do you."

Connor shrugged his shoulders. "In my case maybe it was karma paying me a visit. Maybe that marriage was my punishment, for what I put you and all the woman in my past through. I'm so sorry."

"At least you're man enough to take responsibility." Thuy said. "And by the way, don't punish yourself forever. You have to forgive yourself."

"I wish, I would've been there that night to save you. I knew Jeromy was a fuck nigga from the moment I laid eyes on his bitch

220

nigga ass." Connor had the exact same vibe about Jeromy that he did about Levi.

This world is too small. Thuy thought. "You knew Jeromy?"

"Yeah." Connor rolled his eyes. "One of my frat brothers introduced us. They were teammates. There was something about him I didn't like. Something about him screamed bitch nigga tendencies."

"I was so blind." Thuy sighed with shame. "You know what the fucked up part is?"

"What?"

"I'm going through the exact same shit with, Macal. I mean I love the guy, but I don't know how much more I can take."

"Sometimes we have to ask ourselves if it's all worth it." Connor advised.

Thuy, let Connor's expert relationship advice marinate for a bit, before dropping this sad ass topic. "Hey. Enough feeling sorry for ourselves. This is a karaoke bar, let's have some fun!" Thuy flashed a big cheesy smile showing all her teeth.

"Thuy, you're right, let's have some fun." Connor zeroed in at the karaoke machine that was not being used.

"Oh no, we are not!" Thuy read Connor's mind.

"Oh yes, we are." Connor took Thuy by the hand and pulled her on stage.

Connor and Thuy, put on a mediocre concert singing *Ja Rule* songs featuring *Ashanti*. They sung *Always on Time, Happy* by *Ashanti* and *Mesmerize*.

Connor and Thuy, put on a great show. The onstage chemistry they displayed was exhilarating and sexy. They hyped up the crowd, everybody was so into the performance they took pictures and recorded it on their phones, including Lady-T.

Jamila

Chapter 50

"Why do you think she wants to see us?" Vida asked Bryn as they approached the front door.

"I don't know, but we're about to find out." Bryn rang the doorbell waiting for an answer. "Hey girl."

"Hey y'all." Tylisha greeted. "Come in." She let Vida and Bryn into the house. After Tylisha married Enzo she and the kids moved in his house.

"Since Enzo took Amery to New York for a retreat at Julliard and Milton took the kids out of town to visit his sister, I have the house to myself. That gives me time to share some things with you two." Tylisha offered Bryn and Vida a seat on the couch in the living room.

"What did you wanna share with us?" Vida asked.

Tylisha sat in a chair and began her spill. "Before I get started let me set something straight. I'm not trying to defend, Macal. I love him, I know he loves, Thuy, but he's an idiot. We can all agree on that."

"Yeah!" Bryn and Vida agreed.

"The reason I asked y'all here, is because I need your help. To save my brother and Thuy from that bitch, Lolette." Tylisha said. "I refuse to stand idly by and watch that hoe ruin my brother's life. I also know y'all don't wanna see her ruin your friend's life either."

"You have our attention." Bryn said.

He and Vida couldn't stand, Lolette. Whatever Tylisha had to say they were all ears if it would help save their friend.

"That bitch is a piece of work. More than you know. Y'all have no idea how grimey this hoe really is." Tylisha said.

"Exactly, how grimey?" Vida asked.

"You know Macal, used to be married, right?" Tylisha reminded.

Bryn went on to answer. "Yeah, to that Fallon chick Thuy ran into. She's locked up at Wadley for causing Macal and Lolette's accident."

"That's right. What y'all don't know is that Fallon and Lolette, were best friends since their childhood in Columbus, Georgia." Tylisha revealed.

What the fuck. Bryn and Vida shared the exact same thought.

"Say what now?" Vida wanted to be completely sure.

"Yes." Tylisha confirmed. "That hoe was fucking Macal, while smiling in Fallon's face. Being the fake ass, ratchet, bitch that she is."

"I can understand why she snapped." Bryn said.

"I don't know why the fuck Macal, is addicted to that bitch." Tylisha said with disgust. "His ass is so addicted, I had to literally pull that nigga out of her worn out pussy the day of the wedding."

Vida couldn't believe this crazy ass shit. "You have gotta be fucking kidding me?"

"I wish I was. I can still smell that nasty, ass, sex filled hotel room." Tylisha shivered at the vivid memory. "And that bitch didn't even bother to wash her ass, before the wedding to perform her maid of honor duties. Coming up there all sweaty and smelling like cologne and shit. She was practically bragging about fucking Macal in Fallon's face."

"What a bitch!" Bryn exclaimed.

"A nasty ass bitch at that!" Vida added to the insult.

"I always find it funny when she get all mad and jealous about Macal fucking other hoes." Tylisha laughed and Bryn and Vida joined in.

"She was in her feelings about not being the only number two, huh." Vida chuckled.

"And her ass had the nerve to hit on Enzo and talk slick shit about me to him, while I was getting ready for our first date." Tylisha said.

"I hope you tore that ass up." Bryn said.

"I couldn't, my babies were in the house." Tylisha said.

"Oh yeah." Byrn understood.

"Go on." Vida said to Tylisha.

"Of course, you know Fallon found out about the affair." Tylisha said.

"How did she find out?" Bryn asked.

Addicted to the Drama 2

Tylisha continued with the tragic story of Macal and Fallon. "After Fallon's by chance run in with Thuy, she decided to surprise him at his office. She caught them in the act. She ran off and ended up falling down the stairs. She had to be rushed to the hospital, and ended up miscarrying."

"That's terrible." Vida's heart went out to Fallon.

"Here's the crazy part. Fallon automatically forgave Macal." Bryn and Vida had looks on their faces, that read where the fuck they do that at, Tylisha understood their reactions. "I know, Enzo, I thought the same thing."

"Did Fallon forgive Lolette that fast?" Vida asked.

"Fuck no." Tylisha answered. "When Lolette showed up at the hospital—"

"Whoa, wait a minute!" Bryn interrupted. "Lolette, actually showed up at the hospital?"

"Yes, that hoe, had the balls she wished she could suck to show her face." Tylisha recapped the hospital scene. "I mean this bitch was trying to push Fallon's buttons. Trying to make her snap. We all tried to calm her down and restrain her, because she needed to recuperate." We tried to get Lolette, to leave, but she kept on taunting Fallon on the sly."

"What made Lolette, come to her senses and leave the hospital?" Vida asked.

"I beat that ass." Tylisha answered without a shred of regret or remorse.

"You go girl!" Bryn and Vida cheered giving Tylisha high fives.

"And you know this." Tylisha boasted.

Tylisha filled them in on the accident. Why Fallon had to be institutionalized. The divorce settlement and how she and the kids visited her. Tylisha, even told them about their childhood and their parents' deaths. She shared that information in order to help them better understand Macal.

"Everything aside, I love Macal and Thuy, I know y'all do too. And just like y'all, I don't want this nasty, sleazy ass, thot to win." Tylisha said.

Jamila

"No, the fuck we don't." Bryn said.

Tylisha went on to the main reason she invited Bryn and Vida over. "Now about this baby, Lolette, is carrying. Something about that shit ain't right."

"You sound like this one." Vida pointed at Bryn.

Tylisha looked over at Bryn. "Really?"

"Hell yeah. The way she announced her pregnancy and her little disappearing act afterwards. That hoe is up to something." Bryn shared Tylisha's suspicions. "She didn't say shit, about the baby to Macal, before making that dramatic scene."

"We're all on the same page." Tylisha said. "Now all we need to do is figure out Lolette's plan."

"What can it be?" Vida wondered.

"I don't know." Bryn said. "But we need to find out like yesterday, because Thotlette is not gonna destroy our sister."

"Sister." Tylisha mumbled to herself.

The word sister took her back to the night at the hospital. Fallon said something about Lolette, doing something to her sister. Lolette, tried to hide it, but Tylisha saw that for a split second she was spooked. Then Lolette, said something about killing somebody and Fallon flipped out. Like it was some sort of trigger. Those two share explosive secrets about the other.

"Sister, sister." Tylisha's phone started to ring, erasing her thoughts. "Excuse me for a moment." Tylisha answered the phone. "Hey, Milton what's up? What the fuck!" Tylisha's yelling in the phone startled Bryn and Vida. "No—no—no, fuck that I'm on my way!" Tylisha hung up the phone and frantically searched for her keys and purse.

"Are you okay?" Vida asked with concern.

"Tylisha, what's wrong?" Bryn shared Vida's concern.

"Welton's been shot!" Tylisha cried out her answer.

"Oh shit." Vida tried to console Tylisha.

Tylisha was shaking with fear about her, baby boy. Her little prince. "I gotta go to the hospital."

"Hop in my car, we'll take you." Bryn offered. Tylisha was too hysterical to drive. The three hopped in Bryn's SUV.

Vida and Tylisha climbed in the backseat and Bryn took off out of the driveway.

With her eyes swollen with tears, Tylisha, prayed for her child. "God please, let my baby be okay! Please!"

Vida held Tylisha in her arms, comforting her the best she could. "Welton, will be okay Tylisha. He will be just fine."

Jamila

Chapter 51

"I'm sorry I threw up all over you." Thuy apologized.

"You good." Connor would be lying, if he said he wasn't grossed out about his shirt covered with nasty, slimy, stank ass vomit. He knew it was an accident, so he was cool about it.

"Besides I don't think anyone's ever died of being puked on." Connor joked about the situation and the two shared a laugh.

"I guess I drunk more than I thought, huh?"

"You and me both." Connor said, taking off his shirt to reveal his well-toned sexy muscles.

"Are you sure it's okay for me to spend the night here?" Thuy asked to be sure. Connor was nice, but she didn't wanna impose. "You know I can stay at my suite."

"No, fuck that, you're staying here." Connor strongly insisted. "Now let me show you where you'll be staying."

Thuy followed Connor upstairs, into his master bedroom. "This is a nice house." Thuy complimented.

"Thanks." Connor said.

"Here you go." Connor presented his master bedroom, which was off the chain, and pointed towards the door that was on the other side of the room. "The bathroom is over there."

"Thank you so much." Thuy flashed a smile.

"Anytime." Connor said. "You relax and get some sleep. "I'll take the guest room down the hall. If you need anything just holla. I'll be here so fast you won't even have to wait. Now in the mean-time some of us gotta wash our vomit covered shirts and take a long hot shower."

The two laughed and Connor left. Thuy slipped out of her clothes and found a robe to put on. Then her petty senses started to tingle.

"Connor!" She yelled loud enough for the entire world to hear her.

Connor, Sonic dashed up the stairs, into the room like a fire was lit under his ass. "What's up?" He panted.

"Just checking." Thuy flashed a teasing smile.

Jamila

Connor had to laugh at that one. "Girl, you so silly."

"Yeah nigga, wash this while you're at it." Thuy handed Connor her clothes.

"Alright cool." Connor said and left.

Thuy looked in Connor's dresser drawer and found one of his oversized USC T-shirts to put on after her much-needed shower. After all that throwing up she'd done, Thuy didn't wanna stink up Connor's nice thousand-dollar sheets, smelling like rotting shit.

****

The loud, ringing, doorbell woke Thuy up from her peaceful comfortable sleep. The bed felt so good, she didn't wanna get out.

"Connor! Somebody's at the door!" The doorbell kept ringing. Connor was still knocked the fuck out. *That nigga can't hear all that damn ringing? His ass sleeps like a fucking rock!*

Thuy got sick and tired of hearing all the damn ringing and climbed out of bed to answer the door. "Don't bother, I'll get it!" Thuy yelled, as she past the room Connor was sleeping in.

Thuy made it downstairs to the front door. When she opened the door, to see who the door ringing fool was, she almost pissed on herself. The person on the other side of the door, was the last person she expected to see.

"Macal!"

"What the fuck is going on?" Macal growled, barging into the house.

Thuy, still couldn't believe Macal, was right there at this very moment. "What—What—"

On the way to the house, all Macal, could think about was the picture and that video of Thuy singing and dancing all up on some nigga. Now her ass was in his house wearing nothing, but a T-shirt.

"You all up on some nigga and now you over here giving him my pussy!" Macal, accused with rage in his voice, as he showed her the picture and the video.

"Whoa, wait a minute! Let me explain!" Thuy pleaded.

She and Macal were having problems, but at the end of the day, he was still her husband. She didn't want him to get the wrong idea.

"Explain what? Why the fuck are you in his house? Wearing nothing, but a shirt—his shirt!" Macal grabbed Thuy's arms and roughly yanked her towards him. He stuck his hand between her thighs and let go of her with the look of disgust. "And your ass ain't got on no panties!"

Oh shit. Thuy had to admit this looked very bad.

She knew she didn't do anything wrong, but trying to convince Macal, was a different story. How in the fuck did he get the picture and video? She'd worry about all of that later, but first she needed to calm Macal down.

"Macal, wait a minute, let me explain!"

"All I wanna know is where the fuck that nigga at?" Macal didn't wanna hear shit from Thuy, at that point.

"Baby, just calm down please!" Thuy was in tears trying to explain herself. "I know this doesn't look good, but you gotta calm down, so I can explain and talk about this."

"Thuy, what's going on down there, baby girl?" Connor's voice was heard as he appeared down stairs wearing nothing but his gray sweatpants.

Macal was getting angrier by the second. "Nigga, what the fuck are you doing here with my wife?"

Connor held his hands up in defense. "Look man, you got the wrong idea. Just calm down alright."

Macal rolled up on Connor and got in his face. "Your ass don't need to tell me to do shit nigga!"

Connor tried to be cool about the situation, but he wasn't gonna be disrespected in his motherfucking house. He had no choice, but to bring out his inner gangsta out.

"Look nigga, you need to get the fuck out my house with all that disrespectful, bullshit!" He growled.

"And you don't call fucking my wife disrespectful, nigga?"

Connor put his arm around Thuy's shoulder. "Look, this is my friend, nothing is going on. All I did was take care of her and show her a good time. Unlike your fuck nigga ass, who keeps shitting on her and put a baby in one of your hoes."

Jamila

That did it for, Macal. He punched Connor straight in his jaw. Connor held his jaw for a moment to ease the pain, then threw a right cross to Macal's eye. The two men started exchanging hard punches.

"Stop it, please! Please stop!" Thuy tried to stop the fight, but both men were too busy knocking each other's brains out to listen to Thuy's voice of reason.

Macal, got Connor in the headlock. Connor elbowed Macal, in the ribs and knocked him down. The men wrestled on the floor, throwing punches both not wanting to back down.

"Stop, please!" Thuy cried.

Connor broke free from Macal's grasp and Thuy, took the opportunity to pull him away, into the kitchen area. She went into the refrigerator to get some ice, put it in a zip lock bag and wrapped a towel around it.

Thuy applied the ice pack on Connor's bruised jaw. "Are you, okay?"

"I'm good." Connor breathed heavily. "I'm so sorry about all of this." He apologized. He didn't mean for the fight to go down, or for Thuy to get caught in the middle. She didn't deserve this.

"There's no need for an apology." Thuy continued nursing his wounds. "You have nothing to be sorry for. Thanks for everything."

Macal, was standing there witnessing his wife, caring for another nigga, while he was all bruised up. Acting like he didn't fucking exist. She had to be fucking him.

Fuck this shit! On that final thought, Macal, walked out of the house and washed his hands completely.

Chapter 52

"Here you go, daddy." Tori dropped off a takeout bag for Olson at his new home.

"Thanks, baby." Olson gave his daughter a kiss on the cheek and proceeded to eat his meal.

"How are you loving your Mercedes?"

"I'm loving it, thanks, baby girl."

"Don't thank me, thank, Thuy." Tori took out her phone and scrolled through the pictures she took of Thuy's financial records.

Tori looked through the information thinking about her next move. Lady-T already filled her in on Macal's impromptu trip to L.A.

"Sorry, I'm late." Jett said as he entered the house. He hugged his sister and gave his father dap. "How much are we getting from, Thuy?"

"Lady-T strongly suggested not to get credit cards, the bank account is all setup, and she spoke with Jeromy." Tori took an envelope out of her purse and handed it to Jett. "Here you go."

"Oh shit!" Jett gushed at the sight of the fat stack of dollar bills. "Are you sure Thuy's gonna take Macal back?"

"Looks like it." Tori said. "They're talking more the last I heard."

"Damn!" Jett exclaimed. "How the fuck, you pulled that off?" He took a seat in the living room, while Olson quietly enjoyed his dinner, and watched TV.

"That shit was too easy." Tori said. "You know what a hopeless, desperate, pathetic romantic that bitch of a half-sister of ours is."

"Right." Jett chuckled.

During a commercial break, Olson turned to Jett and asked. "How's my future grandbaby doing?"

Jett blushed at the thought of being a daddy. "The baby is fine. Lolette, called and told me the appointment went well."

"Good." Tori said with a smile.

Not only were they gonna clean Thuy out, they were also gonna

Jamila

trick her, and her philandering husband into raising an outside baby that wasn't even his.

Chapter 53

Thuy rushed back to Atlanta as soon as she could. She tried calling and texting Macal, but no luck. She gave up after the fifth time being sent to voicemail. She didn't know who to turn to. Her friends were nowhere to be found. So, she went to the only other place she could go without receiving judgement, but instead unconditional love and comfort.

"I don't get it, momma." Thuy cried in Isla's arms, in her guest bedroom. "He wouldn't even let me explain, he just left me. Why would he think I'd cheat on him?"

"I'm sorry, baby." Isla comforted her daughter.

"Why? I mean I put up with all his mess. I'm trying to make a legitimate effort to deal with Lolette's baby drama, and he has the nerve to question my loyalty. It ain't right."

"I know it ain't right, but that's how men are setup." Isla said. "They can't stand to see their woman entertaining another man." Thuy tried to explain herself again, but Isla cut her off. "I know you said nothing happened between you and Connor and I believe you. No matter how innocent or guilty it looks, men don't wanna hear it when they get jealous and angry. All they see is red."

"But what about all that cheating he was doing and now he has a baby on the way?"

"It doesn't matter, men have fragile egos." Isla shook her head. "A man can fuck a hundred hoes and you can forgive him every time. Hell, less than a minute after leaving another bitch's house. If that man finds out his woman, even so much as said hi to another man. He'd flip the fuck out and wanna call it quits without any explanation or considering working it out."

"That doesn't make any sense." Thuy wiped away her tears.

"When do men ever make sense?" Isla half joked.

"I heard that!" Greg appeared in the doorway taking offense to his wife's comment.

"Nigga nobody's talking to your ass." Isla playfully snapped at Greg with a smirk.

"Uh huh." Greg went over to Isla and pulled her in his arms, grabbing her ass. "We gonna see who runs shit."

Isla giggled, the two made out like they were about to fuck right there.

That was Thuy's cue to quickly pull herself together and go home.

"Thanks for the talk momma. I gotta go."

"Are you sure you don't wanna spend the night to clear your mind?" Isla asked.

Fuck no! I don't wanna hear that nasty ass shit. "I'm good. My mind is clear enough. Goodnight."

Thuy bid Isla and Greg goodnight, then took off for home to avoid being subjected to hearing the noises of their fuck session. Hopefully, Macal has calmed down enough to talk. After all the shit he'd put her through he at least owed her that much.

****

Thuy was tired and sleepy as fuck. She couldn't wait to get home. Macal might have been sleep by now. The plan was to crash on the couch in the living room and talk things out in the morning.

Thuy parked the car in the driveway. She had her key handy ready to enter the house. She tried putting her key in the lock to open the door, but it didn't fit. That was strange. Maybe she put it in wrong. She tried it again. Still no luck.

"What the fuck?"

Thuy took a good look at her key and the lock and quickly figured out why her key didn't work. "No know this nigga didn't." *That petty motherfucker.*

Thuy paced up and down the front porch in frustration and annoyance. "That motherfucker locked my black ass out of our motherfucking house!"

Thuy's first instinct was to knock down the damn door, like she was the motherfucking police trying to bust a trap house, but decided against it. That method was too easy and predictable. She had to make Macal think he got away with the shit as she made her move.

236

Thuy dug in her purse and took out two bobby pins. She looked at the lock and shaped the pins to match the keyhole. She stuck the pins in the keyhole and picked the lock successfully on the first try.

The advantage of having a career criminal for a big brother. Thuy congratulated herself and entered the house. She creeped up the stairs quiet as a mouse. She made sure not to make any noise.

"Ah, ah, oh shit!" Lolette's loud moans of pleasure were heard coming from the master bedroom.

Thuy knew what was going on, but she had to see the shit for herself. She approached the bedroom she shared with her husband and took an inconspicuous peek inside. There was her husband fucking the shit out of Thotlette in their marital bed. The ultimate disrespect anyone could do to their spouse.

Watching them going at it made Thuy's heart crumble. Locking her out the house and bringing a whore, who had caused nothing but trouble in their lives, to fuck in their home and their bed. All to get Thuy back for her alleged infidelity.

"That's it baby. Nut on this dick. Make it wet baby!" Macal grunted as he busted up Lolette's walls. "I love you, baby girl!"

"I love you too, baby!" Lolette screamed with pleasure, kissing Macal while busing another nut.

Hearing the word love used between Macal and Lolette killed, Thuy, on the inside. She'd seen and heard enough. She lost all the fight she had left inside her. How could Macal throw their love and marriage away so quickly and easily? Thuy didn't know why and at that moment she didn't care. She quietly walked back downstairs without interrupting them.

Thuy was about to walk out the house in devastating defeat, but something came over her. She was Thuy Mackenzie Ellis-Kilborn. Daughter of Isla Jesse Ellis-Dawson and Ellis girls weren't no punks. Thuy was not about to go out like no sucka.

Thuy went into the kitchen to grab some notebook paper from one of the drawers, a black magic marker and tape. She took the pieces of paper and wrote the following lines on each piece of paper:

•*I'm not one of your fans!*

Jamila

- *Don't fuck with me fellas.*
- *This ain't my first time at the rodeo!*
- *No wire hangers!*
- *Bring me the axe!*
- *The sword cuts both ways!*
- *Why must everything be a contest*
- *I'm not mad at you, I'm mad at the dirt!*
- *When you polish the floor, you have to move the tree!*

Afterwards, Thuy taped the pieces of paper all over the living room to let Macal, know she was there. She left the house without bothering to close the door behind her. She got in her car and started driving without a fucking clue where she was going. Thuy, was completely drained. She was all cried out. All tried out. All fought out. The song playing on the way to Thuy's unknown destination was *I'm Outside Hoe* by *D.S.G.B.*

All during the drive, Thuy, replayed her entire drama filled marriage.

"That nigga fucking around on me. Having all those bitches in my face. Wouldn't check Thotlette! Getting her ass pregnant. Got the nerve to question my motherfucking loyalty."

Thuy was fuming like a ball of fire. "I've been taking his foul, ass shit all this motherfucking time and now he wanna shut my ass out and replace me with that bitch. No fucking wa—"

A big truck rammed Thuy's car from behind so hard causing her to lose control and hit a light pole. The light pole then fell on top of her car.

The driver took a picture of the gruesome accident and sent it via text message along with a message that read:

It's done! to Lady-T and drove away leaving an unconscious, Thuy, stuck in her extremely totaled car with no way out.

TO BE CONTINUED...
Addicted to the Drama 3

Submission Guideline.

Submit the first three chapters of your completed manuscript to ldpsubmissions@gmail.com, subject line: Your book's title. The manuscript must be in a .doc file and sent as an attachment. Document should be in Times New Roman, double spaced and in size 12 font. Also, provide your synopsis and full contact information. If sending multiple submissions, they must each be in a separate email.

Have a story but no way to send it electronically? You can still submit to LDP/Ca$h Presents. Send in the first three chapters, written or typed, of your completed manuscript to:

LDP: Submissions Dept
Po Box 870494
Mesquite, Tx 75187

DO NOT send original manuscript. Must be a duplicate.

Provide your synopsis and a cover letter containing your full contact information.

Thanks for considering LDP and Ca$h Presents.

Jamila

Addicted to the Drama 2

TRAPHOUSE KING

By **Hood Rich**

BLAST FOR ME **II**

RAISED AS A GOON **V**

BRED BY THE SLUMS **III**

By **Ghost**

A DISTINGUISHED THUG STOLE MY HEART **III**

By **Meesha**

ADDICTIED TO THE DRAMA **III**

By **Jamila Mathis**

LIPSTICK KILLAH II

By **Mimi**

THE BOSSMAN'S DAUGHTERS 4

WHAT BAD BITCHES DO

By **Aryanna**

Available Now

RESTRAINING ORDER **I & II**

By **CA$H & Coffee**

LOVE KNOWS NO BOUNDARIES **I II & III**

By **Coffee**

RAISED AS A GOON I, II, III & IV

BRED BY THE SLUMS I, II

BLAST FOR ME

By **Ghost**

LAY IT DOWN **I & II**

LAST OF A DYING BREED

BLOOD STAINS OF A SHOTTA I & II

By **Jamaica**

LOYAL TO THE GAME

Jamila

LOYAL TO THE GAME II

LOYAL TO THE GAME III

By **TJ & Jelissa**

BLOODY COMMAS I & II

SKI MASK CARTEL

By **T.J. Edwards**

IF LOVING HIM IS WRONG…I & II

By **Jelissa**

WHEN THE STREETS CLAP BACK **I & II**

By **Jibril Williams**

A DISTINGUISHED THUG STOLE MY HEART **I & II**

By **Meesha**

PUSH IT TO THE LIMIT

By **Bre' Hayes**

BLOOD OF A BOSS **I, II, III & IV**

By **Askari**

THE STREETS BLEED MURDER **I, II & III**

THE HEART OF A GANGSTA **I & II**

By **Jerry Jackson**

CUM FOR ME

CUM FOR ME 2

CUM FOR ME 3

An **LDP Erotica Collaboration**

BRIDE OF A HUSTLA **I II & III**

THE FETTI GIRLS **I, II& III**

By **Destiny Skai**

WHEN A GOOD GIRL GOES BAD

By **Adrienne**

A GANGSTER'S REVENGE **I II III & IV**

THE BOSS MAN'S DAUGHTERS

Addicted to the Drama 2

Jamila

By **Misty Holt**

LOVE & CHASIN' PAPER

By **Qay Crockett**

TO DIE IN VAIN

By **ASAD**

BROOKLYN HUSTLAZ

By **Boogsy Morina**

BROOKLYN ON LOCK I & II

By **Sonovia**

GANGSTA CITY

By **Teddy Duke**

A DRUG KING AND HIS DIAMOND

A DOPEMAN'S RICHES

By **Nicole Goosby**

Addicted to the Drama 2

BOOKS BY LDP'S CEO, CA$H

TRUST IN NO MAN
TRUST IN NO MAN 2
TRUST IN NO MAN 3
BONDED BY BLOOD
SHORTY GOT A THUG
THUGS CRY
THUGS CRY 2
THUGS CRY 3
TRUST NO BITCH
TRUST NO BITCH 2
TRUST NO BITCH 3
TIL MY CASKET DROPS
RESTRAINING ORDER
RESTRAINING ORDER 2
IN LOVE WITH A CONVICT

Coming Soon
BONDED BY BLOOD 2
BOW DOWN TO MY GANGSTA

Jamila